These stories are fast paced and high danger. This is my first by Aleckson and it's a great addition to this multi author series. A redemption romance that really had me pondering my own reactions and opinions. I couldn't put this book down and I'm excited for more in this series and from this author.

MICHAELA, GOODREADS

Another amazing addition to the Chasing Fire: Montana series. Get ready for an intense ride with danger, romance, and adventure in the midst of a wildfire.

ALLYSON, GOODREADS

Michelle Sass Aleckson did an excellent job! The suspense, adventure, drama, nailbiting and faith nuggets just upped a level. I could not stop reading until the very last page. What an awesome faith punch: "Forgiveness and mercy can never be earned." All the action and suspense I love but filled with the faith-nuggets I need! It is better than any action tv-series out there! Truth? I would rather read a new release than watch an episode!

CARLIEN, GOODREADS

FLASHBACK

CHASING FIRE MONTANA | BOOK 3

A SERIES CREATED BY SUSAN MAY WARREN AND LISA PHILLIPS

MICHELLE SASS ALECKSON

Flashback
Chasing Fire: Montana, Book 3

Print ISBN: 978-1-963372-13-7
Ebook ISBN: 978-1-963372-12-0

For more information about Michelle Sass Aleckson, please access the author's website at www.michellealeckson.com.

Published in the United States of America.
Cover Design: Lynnette Bonner

To those who bravely and yet so often silently fight the invisible struggles of addiction and mental health challenges. You matter and you are never alone.

This means that anyone who belongs to Christ has
become a new person. The old life is gone;
a new life has begun!
2 Corinthians 5:17 (NLT)

My sin—oh, the bliss of this glorious
thought!—
My sin, not in part but the whole,
Is nailed to the cross, and I bear it no more,
Praise the Lord, praise the Lord, O my soul!

ONE

THESE MOUNTAINS WERE ALLIE MONROE'S LAST hope. They weren't nearly far enough to escape her past, but then again, nothing was. At least here she had the best shot at getting away and focusing on her search and rescue work. It's really all she had, and she'd been out of it for far too long. She'd settle for a good training session with Scout so she could get back to it.

Of course, to do that, her best friend needed to get out of her cozy little bed in the camper next door. Allie might not be able to see the sun dawning on the horizon, with all the trees and the Rocky Mountains in the way, but there was plenty of light to hit the forest trail, even with the haze of wildfire smoke in the air.

Her phone rang. Allie stared at the picture of her mother and father together right outside the church she'd grown up in. Their smiling faces stirred up too much to deal with this early in the morning. She'd have to call her mother later. Or text. Mom would understand. There was too much riding on getting

Scout trained to hear all about how great her siblings were doing at the moment.

She set the prepped backpack by her orange-and-yellow tent while her black Labrador sniffed around the campsite. He followed his nose to the base of a ponderosa pine until the slap of the camper door broke his concentration. He made a beeline for Belle Jamison as she walked toward them.

Finally.

"Ugh. How do you function this early?" Belle's blonde curls escaping from the wide floral headband took the term *bed head* to a new level.

"You're awake." Allie pocketed her phone. "Great. I was thinking—"

"Whoa. Pump the brakes." Belle held up a hand. "I'm here, but I need a shower house visit and a couple mugs of coffee before I'm ready for anything."

Scout whined. Her friend knelt down and scrubbed his neck with both hands. His tail thumped like a jackhammer.

"He's a morning person like you." Belle's groggy voice teased. "No wonder you picked him out."

"Actually, Dani picked him out for me." As one of the lead trainers at the SAR K9 school outside of Benson, Washington, Dani Masterson was who Allie aspired to be. "He's smart, but he's no Dixie. He hardly listens to me on the first go."

"Yeah, but is it even fair to compare the two dogs?"

"I guess not." No animal could replace the sweet golden retriever mix that had stayed loyally by her side for the last seven years. Dixie could practically read her mind.

"You and Dixie just had a special bond. You'll get there with Scout too."

Would she? Her bond with Dixie had been forged by heartbreak and trauma, and even Belle didn't know the whole of it. Allie couldn't go through that again.

She shook the painful memories away.

Scout was intelligent and eager. He had the drive a search and rescue K9 needed, but they still weren't…connecting.

"He needs to trust me. And we should've been at that point months ago."

"Give him time." Belle stood, letting Scout go on exploring. "And I know that's why you're all gung ho about hitting the trail and getting that training done, so why don't you brew us some coffee and I'll be back in a jiff." She walked away toward the shower house in her flip-flops and pajama shorts.

Right. Coffee. And probably she should feed her dog. "Scout, come."

He glanced her way for a second, then went back to sniffing out what was probably a chipmunk trail. He lifted a back leg and left his mark.

"Gee, thanks." She stifled the sigh that rose. How exactly did Dani get him to listen to her? She could whisper a command at the training school, and Scout would immediately follow it and beg for more.

She tried a slightly higher voice. "Ready for breakfast?"

At that, she had all his attention. Scout trotted over and sat at her feet.

"Oh, sure. You come on the first call if it's got to do with food, huh?"

She scooped food into his collapsible camping

bowl. "Eat up now. As soon as Belle is back and properly caffeinated, she'll hide out in that big forest, and you get to find her."

He didn't bother looking up at her as he dug into his kibble.

"I know you hear me." She just didn't understand why he didn't *listen* to her. They needed that figured out by the end of this five-day trip.

She'd already missed so many opportunities. Opportunities to help find the lost. God couldn't possibly expect her to sit around doing nothing while she had the resources to help.

It was going to be a hot one though. Even in her light trail pants and moisture-wicking tee, she was sweating. The air was heavy with smoke. She'd had to fight to find a cancellation to get this spot when she'd reserved it last month, but a good chunk of the campsites remained empty now, thanks to a wildfire outside of Ember. It had already burned hundreds of acres, but it seemed to be contained for the moment, according to the last report she'd found. It kept her friend Emily Micah, a hotshot firefighter, too busy to meet up with, but that was okay since Allie was here to train Scout.

He finished his breakfast and went back to sniffing around the trees.

Allie dug through her supply tote for the percolator and coffee grounds.

"Nice doggie!" A little boy in a striped shirt and floppy-rimmed explorer hat left the campground gravel road and crossed the sandy dirt to approach her useless campfire ring. With the burn ban, it was propane fuel only for heating up her water.

He reached out to pet Scout.

"Nolan, you shouldn't pet a strange dog without asking." An older boy—probably a brother, given the similar blue eyes and tawny blond hair—pulled the younger one away.

Allie smiled at the boys. "It's okay. You can introduce yourselves if you like. Let him smell you." The boys moved closer. Allie knelt by Scout and held his collar. "This is Scout and I'm Allie."

Nolan squatted in front of Scout, who proceeded to lick a sticky purple smear off the boy's cheek. The older brother stuck a hand out in Allie's direction. "I'm Ethan. This is my brother Nolan."

Allie shook the proffered hand. "Nice to meet you."

"We're here for the weekend. We're over there with the blue tent." He pointed a few spots down the way with a black truck parked next to the metal fire ring.

"And where are you off to so early? You look like you're ready for an adventure." Their tent was zipped up, no adults in sight.

"We wanna get another hike in before we hafta go home."

"Alone?" The older boy could've been nine or ten, but his younger brother looked like he was barely in kindergarten.

"We've been here a bunch of times. I keep Nolan safe. And we always have our survival packs." He pointed to his rather full backpack.

"What about your parents? Do they know you're going on a hike?"

Ethan balked. "Of course my mom knows. We do this all the time."

Nolan stopped petting Scout long enough to nod.

"That's pretty…brave."

Ethan pulled his shoulders back and puffed out his chest a little.

"Ethan knows these trails real good. And he is super-duper brave. Like when we hided and runned away from that bad man, or when Ray tells scary stories about grizzly bears or ghosts. He never gets scared." Nolan moved over and grinned up at his big brother.

But wait—

"A bad man? On the trail?" Allie asked them.

Ethan elbowed his little brother. "He's just making that up. Like the ghost stories. Right, Nolan?"

Nolan's face scrunched up. "We saw that scary—"

"Bear. Yeah, we saw the bear, but it was a black bear. Not a grizzly. And it was far away." Ethan backed away, pulling Nolan with him. "We better go if we want to do the Green Hiking Loop. Mom said we're leaving after lunch. And you know Ray hates it if we're late."

Something flashed in the little boy's eyes, but it dissolved into giggles when Scout gave him one more lick. "Okay. Bye, Scout! I'll come say goodbye before we go home!"

The boys skipped off in the hazy air. Oh, to be carefree and excited like a child. Following the siren call of adventure and imagination only caused trouble. Trouble she was still paying for every day.

But she wasn't their parent.

And didn't that send a shaft of pain straight to her heart.

If their mother was okay with them hiking alone, hopefully they'd be all right. But she couldn't quite settle the unease in her middle as she watched them go off down the gravel road.

The Green Hiking Loop.

Maybe that's where they should do their training this morning. Just in case.

Allie went back to her burner and lit the blue flame under the percolator.

"I hope my boys weren't bothering you." The woman who walked into Allie's campsite was young and pretty, with wavy brunette hair pulled back in a ponytail and dark brown eyes. Eyes acquainted with hardship, giving her an older appearance.

Because of Ray and his scary stories, maybe?

"Ethan and Nolan? They just wanted to meet Scout here." Allie nodded toward the Lab, who had already trotted over to the woman and sniffed her boots. "They weren't a bother."

"Good."

"I'm Allie."

The woman made no move to come closer, keeping her gaze directed at Scout and offering him some scratches behind the ears. He leaned into her legs as if he couldn't get enough.

Huh. He never did that for Allie.

Even a perfect stranger had a better bond with her dog. But who was she?

"What's your name again?" Allie asked.

"Oh, I'm Jen." She didn't quite meet Allie's eyes as she gave a tremulous smile in her direction. Must be shy. Her boys certainly weren't though.

"So, the boys were off to hike the Green Loop. They must be pretty experienced to go by themselves."

"They're in Boy Scouts. They know these trails

since we're here so often. I can hardly keep up with them anymore."

"You're not afraid of wild animals or something happening to them? I'm an SAR worker, so I get a little paranoid, I admit. But they mentioned a scary man."

Jen's eyes widened for a nanosecond. It was so slight Allie almost didn't see it as Jen quickly laughed and waved her hand, as if pushing Allie's concern aside. "Oh, the boys love telling stories. I blame my husband. He's always riling them up with ghost stories and the like. They always try to outdo him. And they have such vivid imaginations at this age."

But following a flight of fancy could have dangerous consequences. How could this woman so flippantly let the boys go gallivanting off in the woods?

Hopefully Belle would be back soon, and they wouldn't be too far behind the boys.

Before she could ask anything more, Jen stuffed her hands in her jean pockets. "I better get back. We leave soon, and it's easier to pack everything without the boys' help."

She gave a half-hearted smile and walked away. Walked away in her dark jeans and a flannel shirt, while Allie was ready to rip off her trail pants and trade them for shorts, except that she didn't want to deal with the mosquito bites, scratches, or ticks once they were in the forest.

"Scout, come." She snapped her fingers.

The Lab looked at her but then focused once more on the woman walking away. Allie called again, this time a little more gusto in the command. Scout whined but obeyed. He was acting strange, even for him. Allie absently stroked his ears as she watched Jen reach her own site.

"Look at you making friends." Belle walked up, hair still wet, but she was dressed for the day in leggings and a long-sleeve tee. "Who was that?"

"Just another camper. Her boys wanted to meet Scout. But she's letting them hike all alone." Allie turned down the flame as the coffee inside bubbled. "I thought we could use the same trail for training this morning. In case they run into trouble."

"Give me some of that coffee you have there, and we can get started."

Belle's phone rang. By the way her eyes lit, it had to be her husband, Matthew. She stepped over toward her camper and answered. Allie focused on the coffee, trying not to eavesdrop on the newlyweds. She tamped down the irritation at yet another delay. She should be grateful she was even able to convince Belle to come with her for the trip when she'd barely left Matthew's .side since the wedding four months ago. But if it was anything like every other phone conversation they'd had, Allie might as well settle in for the long haul.

She glanced at Allie with a forced smile and then pointed toward her camper. "But we just got here last night," Belle said. The door slapped shut behind her.

Yup. This was going to be a while.

But it was only a few minutes before Belle was walking out of the camper with worry lines on her forehead.

"What's going on?" Allie handed her friend a mug of coffee.

"We need to go." Belle sipped her drink.

"I know. As soon as you finish, we can." Allie

whistled to Scout. It took three times, but he finally came and sat at her feet. Reluctantly.

"No, Al. We need to leave. Matthew said that wildfire is too close. He's not comfortable with us being out here."

"But I thought the fire was to the east. I checked yesterday."

Belle shook her head slowly. "It's heading this way. According to what Matt's buddies at the fire department said, he's surprised they haven't issued an evacuation order yet."

"If they haven't issued the order yet, we're fine."

"Maybe, but I told Matt I'd head home today."

"Belle—"

"If he were here and I was back home, I'd want him to leave. I think you and Scout should leave too."

"Leave? Now? We just got here yesterday." She needed training time. This was her chance.

"Why don't you come to Idaho with me? You could see our new place. You haven't been back to Twin Valley in ages."

And be a jolly third wheel to the honeymoon couple? As much as she missed Belle and was happy for her to have found true love, she didn't think she could stomach five days of witnessing their happy lives together and all that Allie would never experience herself. And besides, she couldn't leave knowing the boys were out in the Kootenai National Forest alone.

"Go ahead, Belle. But Scout and I will stay." Allie opened up her backpack, looking for Scout's harness.

"Don't be like that. There's plenty of wilderness where I am—"

"You need to be with Matthew. I get that. But I

can't go. Not yet." Allie slipped Scout's harness on him, focusing on the clip, willing her eyes not to drip the tears stinging them. This was supposed to be time with her best friend. Time together and time to figure out how to get Scout to listen to her.

"Allie, you don't have to do this alone."

"I'm not alone. I have Scout." Allie stood and settled her backpack straps onto her shoulders. She dug up a bright smile for her friend. "It's okay. We'll just stay a day or two, and maybe I'll stop and see you on my way home."

Belle studied her as if sniffing out any sign of caving. With a resigned sigh, her brow relaxed. "Are you sure?"

"Those boys are still out there, and Scout knows their scent. That will be our training today. And if there's any sign of the fire getting close, I'll leave. But for now, I'll stay, and we'll be fine." Allie gave Belle a squeeze. "Really."

"Maybe this will be good. You could hike this morning for fun. Get some *bonding* time with Scout."

Allie quirked an eyebrow. "What exactly are you implying?"

"It's just...I've seen you with Scout now, and I don't think he has a listening problem. I think you two haven't bonded yet, and it's because you're holding back."

Allie folded her arms across her chest. "I have spent every waking hour of the last few months with that dog."

Belle didn't stand down. She met Allie's stare-down with a pointed look of her own. "You spend a lot of time with him, yes. But you barely touch him. You talk to him only when it's something you need him to do. And I haven't seen you once smile or look at him like you actually like him. Like you would with Dixie—"

"Let's not go there." Allie clenched her teeth together tight, willing the emotions clogging her throat to stay down and not leak out.

Belle must've gotten the message. "So you're not ready to talk about that. Fine. But I'm here for you when you are." She wrapped her arms around Allie's stiff shoulders. "Al, come with me. Please."

Allie allowed herself to relax a fraction and lean into her friend's embrace. "I love you, Belle, but you belong with Matthew." And she belonged…well, nowhere, really. Not that she had anyone but herself to blame. "You should get going." She pulled away and stood tall.

"What about your family? They miss you."

"I talk to them all the time." With her six siblings, it tended to be more texts, but still. She stayed in touch. "Mom and Dad call weekly."

"Calls that I've heard tend to go to voicemail or are cut short."

"I can't help that they always call while I'm busy."

"Which is exactly why you should come with me. You can have some quality time with me *and* your parents."

"My job is riding on this. I have to stay."

"There's nothing I can say that will convince you to leave?"

"You know me better than that." Allie tried on a smirk. She didn't need Belle worrying about her.

Belle chuckled as she rolled her eyes. "Yeah, I do. But first, I think I have enough time to cook you a real breakfast instead of one of those gross protein bars you're so fond of."

As much as she wanted to hit the trail, she wouldn't begrudge one last meal with her BFF.

They lingered over their pancakes and bacon—Belle always did have a knack for pancakes—but eventually Allie helped her friend unhook the lines to the camper and pack her little Subaru.

Belle headed toward Allie's tent. "We should get you packed up and ready to go."

More delays. "That's okay. You should hit the road. I know Matthew is texting you."

Belle's sheepish grin said she'd guessed right. "Yeah, but you helped me. I can—"

"It's a little tent. It won't take long. You should get back to your husband." Allie steered Belle toward the car.

"All right. But promise me you will get everything ready. And you'll come visit me on your way to Benson."

"Of course."

Allie pushed away the disappointment of the ruined trip and put on as cheerful a face as she could muster to wave goodbye when Belle pulled out. True to her word, she took her own tent down and packed all her belongings in her SUV.

Finally, she clipped the lead on Scout's harness, ready to track the two boys on the Green Hiking Loop. They were probably back by now, but Scout could still follow their trail.

"Come on, Scout. Let's go for a hike."

She took two steps before a fire truck pulled into the campground, lights flashing.

A loud voice from a speaker called out. "This is

Jude County Hotshots. Please evacuate the campground as quickly and safely as possible."

This wasn't how it was supposed to be. But any former addict knew life didn't always go the way it should.

Any cop knew a situation could go sideways fast—especially in SWAT situations.

For hotshot firefighter Dakota Masterson, a guy who had been both those things—and still was—the fight to prove himself didn't look much like battling wildland flames.

Right now it looked like riding around in the truck with two other crewmates, including Houston James, who was asking a whole lot of personal questions.

It must be the youth pastor in him. That drive to get to know people.

Dakota liked the guy. He really did. He appreciated that they shared a faith and all, but he was asking about Dakota's past.

And that just wasn't gonna fly.

He was a *new* man. That's what Preach always said in their morning Bible studies this last year. So, no need to drag out all his dirty laundry in front of this new team. Commander Miles Dafoe knew the gist of it, but no one else did. Which was how it should be.

They didn't have to know about him getting kicked off the SWAT team, the stint in rehab, or any of it. This was his fresh start. No more depending on his big brother Will Masterson, former federal agent, and his perfect reputation to help Dakota move up in the world. He would do that with hard work and by the sweat of his brow. Literally. And the sign-on bonus would help him pay Will back every cent he'd spent on the Ridgeman Center.

For now, Dakota would keep a tight lid on his ugly past. Although, if anyone understood, it might be these guys. Between Hammer and his big "trouble" tattoo and Kane and his somewhat melancholy personality, they probably all had ghosts of the past they wrestled with. But they barely knew each other. It was one thing to have his former boss, Gage Deluca, checking in with him, asking about his addiction. If these guys knew, he'd probably lose what little connection he'd already forged with them.

So how much longer before he could put boots on the ground and get out of this conversation?

Kane drove the truck through the campground, also avoiding the conversation. But Houston still craned his body around from the passenger side, looking at Dakota. Waiting.

"So, Masterson, what was it that made you switch from SWAT to hotshot again?"

"Guess it's my turn now." Dakota grabbed the speaker from the middle console and tried for a playful grin. "This is the Jude County Hotshots firefighter crew. Please evacuate the campground as quickly and safely as possible. This is a mandatory evacuation."

He peered out the windows as they rolled down the winding road through the big campground dotted with tents and campers and surrounded by towering pines. "I still can't believe there's this many people here. This is going to take a while."

Finally, the truck in front of them stopped. "Looks like we're ready to start knocking on campers."

And that was just fine with him.

Kane brought the truck to a halt, and they piled out. The man didn't talk a whole lot. Usually got right to the point and spent the rest of the time brooding. But he was quick on his feet and strong. Not a bad kind of guy to have as a partner. He'd have to make sure he stuck with Kane for whatever assignment came next and avoid Houston.

The three men approached the hotshots leader, Conner Young, and the others gathered around him.

"Masterson and Kane, catch up with Emily and take sites two hundred to three hundred. James, go with Sax and Sanchez and take the four hundreds spots on this loop. The others are covered."

Whew. Houston would go with the quiet Saxon and prickly Sanchez. Maybe he could use his youth pastor skills and figure out whatever it was that made the Latina woman walk around like she was angry with the world.

Dakota and Kane walked past the few empty campsites. Smoke hung thick in the air. Why would anyone *want* to stick around in this? But tents and RVs still remained. Kane and Dakota walked up to the first RV and knocked on the door.

An older man in a Hawaiian shirt answered. "Yeah, yeah, I know. I heard ya. We're packing."

"Sorry to disturb you, sir. And make sure you avoid the highway south. They're detouring everyone west."

The man nodded. "Understood." With the slap of the screen door, they were dismissed.

Alrighty then.

The next few sites were vacant. Emily Micah stood talking to a woman by a yellow-and-orange tent. Something about the woman was familiar, but her back faced Dakota. She was petite with medium-length, sable-brown hair pulled back into a ponytail. A black Lab on a lead sniffed Emily's boots.

Why did something about the stranger stir his memory, like he knew her? He didn't know anyone with a dog like that.

The woman turned to call the dog, her profile now in view.

No. It couldn't be.

Here? In the middle of nowhere? He'd thought—okay, he'd hoped—he would never see her again. But was it even the same woman from over a year ago, the one who'd driven him from Benson, Washington, to Last Chance County for rehab?

Didn't that just beat all? He'd come to the wilderness—where no one would know him—for a fresh start, and here was Allie Monroe, whose *only* connection to him was the fact that she knew his brother and had driven him to rehab. And she was already talking to Emily.

"You comin' or what?" Kane, having walked on, looked back at him.

And have to talk to her? "Ya know, why don't we split up? I'll cut across and start over—"

"Oh no. You're the smooth talker. I'm the intimidation. Besides, looks like Emily found a friend I wouldn't mind being introduced to."

Right. Because Allie did have rather alluring hazel eyes. Eyes that had never once judged him, despite seeing him at his absolute worst. And she *was* beautiful.

But she could also destroy everything he was building here with a few words.

Dakota attempted to tamp down the unease in his middle as he followed Kane. This was what he got for wanting to keep the past in the past. He should've known he could never outrun it.

Maybe Allie wouldn't remember him. They'd only met once.

Then again, they'd spent eight hours in that car together. Of course she was going to remember him.

The problem was, would she blab it all or keep his past to herself?

"Emily, who did you find?" Gone was Kane's usual brooding face. He flashed Allie a smile he must keep only for pretty women, because this was the first Dakota was seeing it.

He tried to keep his face down by petting the dog that came to check him out. But wait, she'd had a different dog last time. A golden retriever.

Emily said, "This is—"

"Dakota?"

Shoot. She remembered all right. Dakota looked up from the dog licking his fingers.

Allie's hazel eyes widened. "It is you."

What did that mean?

"Wait. You guys know each other?" Emily asked.

"Met last year," Dakota spat out quickly before Allie could say anything about the circumstances of that meeting. "How have you been?"

"Fine." Given the look on her face, he wasn't sure that was the truth. "What are you doing here?"

She thought he should still be in rehab or something? "I'm with Jude County Hotshots." He looked back at the black Lab. "Where's Dixie?"

"She—" Her voice caught. "Um, she was hit by a car."

Dakota rubbed against the ache in his chest. Allie had loved that dog. And of course he had to bring up all that pain. "I'm so sorry."

"It's okay." She attempted a smile, but it didn't quite reach. "You didn't know."

The Lab moved from Dakota to Kane, begging for more attention, by the looks of it, as it pawed Kane's leg. The broody glare Kane typically wore was nowhere to be found. Huh.

"So, who is this?" Dakota asked her.

"This is Scout. We're doing some training exercises so I can get back to my SAR work."

Good. The tight muscles across his abdomen relaxed a bit. If she wasn't here in an official capacity, she'd have to follow the evacuation orders and had no choice but to leave. As much as he might want to help her process more through the loss of Dixie and see how she was *really* doing, she was the one person here who knew why he'd left Benson. And he didn't need that spread around his new team.

It was hard to start a new life when the old one wasn't too far behind, constantly haunting him and trying to trip him up. He wanted to be the man God wanted him to be, and that meant reinventing himself. Wasn't that one of the verses they'd learned, something about forgetting the past and straining toward the goal?

So, time to say *adios* to Allie and her glaring ties to that past. No matter how alluring those eyes still were.

Dakota tried for a charming smile to soften the blow. "I'm sorry to cut your trip short, but you and

Scout will have to leave. There's a mandatory evacuation."

Emily swung around and stared at him. "It's not like Allie is some green tourist. She'll be okay if she sticks close to us while we clear everyone else out. We might need a search and rescue team."

Dakota pressed his lips together and stared at Emily instead of saying what he wanted to. "I'm sure she has better things to do. There's got to be other places to train." He tried to keep a pleasant expression and turned away.

"Actually, I'd rather stick around and help. Scout needs all the experience he can get."

He winced and glanced over his shoulder to see her sharing a smile with Kane. That was the very last thing he needed. "Don't you think it would be better to go somewhere safer?"

She glared at him. Probably knew he was trying to get rid of her—just not for the reasons she thought. "I'll be f—"

"Allie?" A woman in flannel ran up to them, stumbling, her face red and fear in her eyes. Emily caught her arms and held her steady. The woman gasped. "Did you see the boys?"

Boys? Who was this lady?

Allie shook her head. "I haven't seen them."

The woman wrung her hands together. "They're missing!"

TWO

ALLIE COULDN'T BELIEVE DAKOTA MASTERSON WAS here in the middle of the Montana wilderness. Clearly he'd succeeded in rehab. His blue eyes were clear and focused—nothing like the bloodshot, full-of-shame look they'd carried last time she'd seen him. Even in sooty pants and a loose T-shirt he looked good. Healthy.

But why he was trying to get rid of her and acting all embarrassed when obviously he should be celebrating wasn't something she had time to figure out. Not when the mother of those two adorable boys looked like she was about to faint.

"I haven't seen Ethan and Nolan since this morning."

Jen sucked in a short breath. "They said they wanted to hike the Green Loop trail, right? That's what they told you?"

Allie nodded.

"They should've been back by now." Jen's voice shook. "And Ray is ready to go, but—" She bit down on her lip like she was trying not to cry. She whipped her head around, looking in every direction, and gasped. "I can't find them."

Allie laid a gentle hand on Jen's arm. "I'm sure they're around. I'll help you look."

No way would Allie leave when two young boys were lost in the forest. So whatever mystery there was to solve about Dakota showing up as a firefighter—a hotshot and part of her friend Emily Micah's crew, no less—needed to wait.

"You need to evacuate, Allie," Dakota said. "It's not safe here."

"Excuse me, this is what I do. I find lost people. Remember?"

Emily gave Dakota a good glare. "Masterson, she's right. We have work to do. We need to finish evacuating. I trust Allie will stay safe. Tho—"

"Jen!" an angry voice yelled. "Where are they?" A bald man, stocky and tall with a bushy beard, came from behind the tent the boys had pointed out that morning. The glower on his face disappeared the moment he spotted them. He walked over with a chuckle. "Sorry to yell, babe. Didn't realize you were visiting with folks." He swung a beefy arm over her shoulders. "Where are the boys? It's time to go, and I bet these firefighters want us out of the way."

Allie watched Jen shrink. "They're still…hiking. I think. I told them to be back by now. Ethan has his watch, but—"

"They aren't back?" The man, presumably Jen's husband Ray, bristled. "We need to get home."

Scout stood at alert, sniffing the man. Unlike he had with everyone else in the group, the Lab didn't go right up to him. Instead, the dog stayed by Allie's side, giving her a solid idea of the dog's instinct about his man—and she got the same vibe.

"I know, but they're missing." Jen's voice hitched.

"Missing?" He looked at Dakota and the guy with him. "You guys are firefighters. Can't you help us find the boys?"

Emily stepped up to him. "We have to finish evacuating, but Allie is a search and rescue professional. She can help find them." She turned to Dakota and his partner. "We better get going. There's still a lot of people, and we need to clear everyone out."

Dakota gaped. "We can't let Allie go alone. The fire is heading right toward the trails."

Jen gasped. "You have to help find them. We have to find them." She looked like she would fall apart any second now.

She would be useless in the forest. This worried mother was the last person who needed to be out with Allie.

She injected as much confidence as she could into her voice. "I need you to stay here in case they come back. If you and your husband search the main campground, check the shower houses and gift shop, and stay here in the central area, I can take Scout and search the trails."

Dakota glared at her. "You shouldn't be out there alone."

"I won't be." Couldn't he see that? "I'll have Scout."

"Yeah, but the fire—"

"Maybe you should go with her," the other firefighter said. What did he say his name was? Kane? "Emily is right. As soon as this place is evacuated, we need to start cutting a break line to save the campgrounds. Gotta keep moving." He nodded to Allie. "If you don't mind, I'm leaving you in good hands." He clapped Dakota on the shoulder and jogged away.

Emily shouted a quick goodbye and warning to be safe.

Great. Now she was stuck with Dakota. Not that she didn't like the guy. She really thought they'd connected at one point, but now he was acting like he wanted to get rid of her. And—yes, maybe the way he'd left with barely a goodbye after that long road trip still stung. But she needed to focus on Jen before she collapsed. She would probably do better with a task. "Jen, Ray, go search those areas I mentioned. One of you stick by the tent. Do you have a phone?"

Jen nodded and pulled her cell out of her back pocket. "Yeah."

Allie gave her her number. "Call if they come back."

Dakota shook his head. "You're not going to have reception out there."

"Maybe not, but I'll check it when I can." Why was he being so difficult?

"Better yet, find one of the other hotshots. Tell them to call me on the radio," Dakota told them.

Jen and Ray rushed off.

Allie swung around to face Dakota. "I'm not the one who needs a babysitter. Don't you have better things to do?"

"There's a fire roaring up this mountain. Like it or not, I'm sticking close by. I can't let you go out there without some protection."

Really? If anything, she might be in more danger *with* Dakota.

His brother Will had insisted that he wasn't violent or anything, but what she'd witnessed the first time they met said otherwise. After the storm of his frustration and anger had blown over, he'd been sullen but peaceful during the long car ride they'd taken together. He'd jokingly warned her that he was trouble with a capital T. But Dani had insisted that Dakota was a good guy. And Dixie had liked him right away. She'd always been a good judge of character.

Man, she missed that dog.

And yeah, maybe Dakota's wounded-hero vibe had seeped through to the long-locked-away places of her heart as they'd passed the hours of that car ride getting to know each other a little. It was a good thing she'd dropped him off at the Ridgeman Center when she did. He'd intrigued her as he'd shared little tidbits of himself.

He liked Garth Brooks and hated sitting in one place too long. He'd grown up in South Dakota and still missed the prairies. He'd made her laugh. Dixie had been downright smitten with him, which told her all she needed to know.

And she'd started to imagine what it would be like to see him again. Get to know him more.

And that was the most dangerous of all.

Her imagination only got her into trouble. She needed her eyes wide open and feet firmly on the ground. Not heady attraction or heated moments. Not with her past.

And something about the combo of brilliant blue eyes in contrast to the red hair and scruff across

Dakota's firm jawline, as well as the strong heroic aura around him, might as well have been a big ol' flashing sign for her.

Warning. Strong attraction potential. Stay far away.

But the facts were glaring. Just when she'd thought they were hitting it off, they'd reached the Ridgeman Center, and he'd waved goodbye and left. No "Hey, could I have your number?" or "Let's keep in touch." Or even a "Thanks for the ride." He'd simply ducked his head and gone through the front doors with barely an acknowledgement of her existence.

Obviously, she couldn't trust herself to read a guy correctly. She too easily saw something when *nothing* was there.

But she also didn't have any training in fighting or avoiding a wildfire. If she wanted to keep the boys safe, she would need Dakota's help.

She crossed her arms, noting, as Scout lay down by Dakota's boots, that even he seemed to like the guy. "Fine, you can come. But I'm leaving now." She swung her backpack over her shoulders and called to her dog. She'd have to work really hard at keeping herself in check with Dakota.

Scout looked up at her but didn't move until she gently tugged on the lead connected to his harness. She could've sworn the dog sighed as he got up and moved to her side.

Dakota didn't seem to notice. "The sooner we find them, the sooner we can get you to a safe place."

"Still acting like a SWAT guy."

His lip curled. "Yeah, well, that life is behind me."

"Is it?" She gave him a pointed look.

A muscle in his jaw twitched. "Let's go find the boys."

So that's how it was going to be. He didn't want to talk about the past. Fine by her. She needed to focus on finding Ethan and Nolan before the fire reached the campground and they couldn't get out.

Allie and Scout jogged up the trail in front of Dakota, almost like she didn't want to be near him.

Guess he couldn't blame her for that. Not with the way they'd met. But like it or not, he wasn't about to let her walk into a forest on fire by herself. Not with the smoke growing thicker by the minute.

The chatter on his radio indicated the fire was headed right for the campground, and the crew was busy trying to dig a break line to protect it.

But fires were unpredictable. All it took was a few sparks—a snag to fall the wrong direction, to cross the barrier the crew was frantically trying to make—and the campground would be consumed.

They needed to find those kids quickly.

But his new life he was trying to build here could also go up in flames just as easily. Being a rookie meant starting all over again. He was breaking new ground on this team. If they heard he was an addict, how he'd let his last team down, it was all over.

So he needed Allie to trust him. And more, to keep his past to herself and not blab it to the crew. Especially if she already knew Emily Micah. And since she worked closely with his sister-in-law Dani, it would go a long way to proving to his brother that his investment in Dakota's rehab hadn't been a waste, that Dakota truly was building a new and better life here.

Could he convince her?

He needed to.

Time to dig up some of that Masterson charm.

"Hey, wait up. I guarantee my pack is heavier than yours." Dakota infused a lightness he didn't really feel into his words.

Allie paused on the trail. Scout continued to sniff. "We need to cover as much ground as we can as quickly as possible. I think Scout has their scent."

"Good." Dakota caught up to her. There was just enough room to walk side by side on the trail. "Did Scout train at the SAR Training Center too?"

"Yeah. We worked with your sister-in-law. She's actually the one that picked out Scout for me."

"How is Dani?"

Allie paused and finally looked at him. "She's good. Have you stayed in touch with her and Will and the boys?"

"Mostly just by email and text."

"Actually, your nephews aren't too far from here. They're at a youth camp farther north."

"Yeah, Sam and Josh told me. So is Scout certified?"

"Not yet. That's why we're here. We're trying to finish his training, but he's proving to be rather stubborn. Well, more stubborn than Dixie ever was for me."

"I'm really sorry about Dixie. I can't imagine how hard it was to lose her."

Allie only nodded. She turned away, eyes scanning the thick forest surrounding them.

Dakota could've palmed his forehead. *Way to make a girl feel comfortable by bringing up her dead dog.*

"Are you still living in Benson?" That was better. Neutral ground.

"Yup." She stopped and pulled her backpack off. "Scout, come. Let's keep you hydrated." The dog didn't listen. Instead he continued up the smoky trail.

"Scout! Come."

This time the black Lab stopped and looked at her, but he still didn't obey her command.

"Come." Allie pulled out a water bottle and collapsible doggie-dish. Finally, Scout trotted back to them and lapped up the water.

"Is that normal for him not to listen the first time?"

Allie glared at him over the water bottle she chugged. "He's still in training."

Lovely. He'd hit another nerve.

But he didn't mind the break from his own pack as he set it on the ground. He and Allie both drank. With this heat, even in the shade of the tall trees, it wouldn't take much to succumb to heat exhaustion. As Allie checked Scout's paws, Dakota studied her.

Thankfully, no signs of paleness or fatigue. Her hair was longer than a year ago, the pointed chin and big hazel eyes exactly the same. Her smooth skin was a dark tan, a shade that seemed to enhance the light color of her eyes—an intriguing mix of amber and jade.

In another life, another situation, he probably would've asked her out. But she barely acknowledged his presence, and he was in no way ready for a relationship.

A year out of rehab? A new job? The timing was all wrong.

"We should get going." He hefted his pack to his shoulders.

Scout lapped up the last of his water and sat on his haunches, watching Allie gather his dish and empty bottle. She didn't acknowledge him.

Weird. With Dixie, she had constantly been talking to her, petting her, giving her lots of attention. But like she'd said, Scout was still training. Maybe this was part of the technique, not to coddle him.

Still, he felt bad for the mutt. Couldn't hurt to give him a little attention while she put things away. Dakota whistled to him. Scout came immediately.

"Hey, you're gonna help us find those boys, right?" Dakota scratched around the dog's ears and collar. Scout leaned into his touch. "Good boy."

Allie slipped her arms through the straps of her own backpack. "Let's go, Scout. Find!"

Scout leaped to his paws and started sniffing, trotting back and forth on the trail.

"He seems like a good dog." Dakota held back an overhanging branch for her.

"He's very driven when he has a scent."

"Why are you training all the way out here? Do you have family in this area?"

"No."

"So..."

She sighed. "I came with a friend. She lives back in our hometown in Idaho, and the plan was to spend some time together, but her husband freaked out about the fire, and she left earlier this morning."

"You're from Idaho, huh? Where abou—"

Allie stopped and faced him. "Look, I know you're

trying to be friendly and everything, but let's not pretend. We're here to find those boys. We'll do the job and go our separate ways again, just like last time." She gave him a tight smile. "This doesn't need to get personal."

But he needed to protect this job. He had Will, Dani, and the boys, but this—this was the one thing he had going for himself, and he couldn't screw that up. She didn't want to be buddy-buddy, fine. But he also needed Allie to see that he was *not* the same guy she'd driven to rehab. He'd have to shoot straight with her.

"You don't trust me, do you?"

Her side-eye glance showed surprise. "I barely *know* you. And what I do know..." Her words trailed off. She shrugged and focused her gaze on Scout up ahead.

Like she didn't want to say what she was really thinking.

He stepped in front of her, forcing her to stop and look at him. "You saw me at my worst. You saw what I did to Will. So I get it. I have no excuse for the things I did then. But that's not who I am now. I'm just asking for a chance."

"A chance at what?"

"To show you that I'm one of the good guys too, like Will. I might not be SWAT anymore or a federal agent like my brother, but I'm trying to build a new life here. I finished my rehab. I'm starting over. So maybe you could help me out. Let me start over with you too."

She stared at him. It wasn't a fast refusal. That was a start.

"I can understand not wanting to be defined by

your past." Her voice was so soft he almost missed her words.

"You've got regrets too, huh?"

Her sharp intake of breath surprised him. "Doesn't everybody?"

He'd only meant to relate, but the grief in her eyes rocked him.

Obviously, he wasn't the only one haunted by his own history. What was Allie hiding?

"But the past is the past, right?" She gave him a tenuous smile, all traces of sorrow swept away. Maybe he'd only imagined it. "And for the record, I've always known you were a hero, Dakota. Just as much as Will is."

Really? Then why did she act so cold with him? "Thanks—"

Her brows furrowed as she looked over Dakota's shoulder.

"What is it?"

"Scout is going off the trail." She jogged after the dog. "Come on!"

Scout led them down a slight incline covered with scrub brush and fallen logs.

"Look!" Allie knelt down in a patch of ferns where Scout sat with his long tongue hanging out as he panted.

She held up a child-size hat. A dark red blob with streaks of mud stained the brim. Studying the ground, Dakota noted a long stretch of bare earth streaking downhill—fresh dirt where someone had fallen and slid.

She looked over with those big eyes. "One of the kids is hurt."

THREE

ALLIE HELD NOLAN'S LITTLE EXPLORER HAT. THEY were on the right track, thank God. But they were far off the trail. Her eyes stung from the growing haze in the air as she strained to see more signs of them.

Why would the boys have left the trail? And who'd fallen and slid so far? It looked like blood on the hat. Her chest squeezed.

Dakota pointed at the hat. "Are you sure that's—"

"Nolan, the younger brother, was wearing this when he came by my campsite this morning."

The boys were out here somewhere. Was it just her, or was it getting harder to breathe?

Without warning, memories battered inside her head. A cold sterile room. Blinding lights glaring down at her.

Dakota's hand rested on her shoulder. She shook off the memories and looked at him.

"You okay?"

She nodded.

He kept his hand on her another moment. She tried not to hate herself for finding comfort in it. She hadn't been lying when she'd said she knew Dakota was a hero. Thanks to his nephews sharing all their "Uncle Kota stories," she knew he'd gone above and beyond when he worked SWAT. He'd put his life on the line for the sake of others, and Will was so proud of him. No wonder she'd felt such an immediate connection with him last year.

But the boys.

"I wonder what they were doing to lose the hat," she said. A hat she should mark. She opened the GPS hiking app on her phone and dropped a pin.

"Not sure. But it looks like one of them, or both of them, slid quite a ways down this incline. I'm going to call this in."

While he talked to his crew on the radio, she knelt by Scout.

"Good job, boy. You're on the right trail." She gave him a little scratch on his chin and offered him more water.

See. She showed him affection. They could... bond.

"We can't stop long. That fire is coming closer. I can hear it now." Dakota turned a slow three hundred sixty degrees.

Sure enough, a dull roaring could be heard through the trees. Allie took a swig of water to wash out the metallic taste of fear, still lingering in her mouth. She quickly finished watering Scout and let him smell the hat. "Find, Scout!"

He took off, bounded over branches and tree roots scattered on the forest floor. Allie and Dakota jogged behind, weaving around thick trunks, skirting the rock outcroppings. There wasn't breath for much conversation now that Scout had the boys' scent. The downward slope made it an easier run but also harder to keep balance. Dakota was nimble enough, even with the heavy pack he carried.

She glanced at him. His red hair peeking out from his helmet stood out among all the green and brown surrounding them. His face was focused, taut. She could easily picture him in his SWAT tactical gear from a picture Will and Dani had displayed with all their family photos. He had probably made a good cop—one who cared about protecting innocents.

His admission about his actions when they met still echoed in her mind.

I'm trying to build a new life here.

I'm starting over. So maybe you could help me out. Let me start over with you too.

Funny how those simple words and his direct gaze bored straight through her defenses.

He wasn't the only one who wanted to rebuild his life.

Who was she to judge? If he knew—if anyone knew…

Stop. Thankfully, they didn't.

She shut down the mental vault inside. It had been too easy to hide because there had been no witnesses. Not when she'd gone to college so far away from home, not knowing anyone. And she hadn't kept up with anyone from that time either. Now she had a job to do in the present. Like Dakota. They both had something to prove.

So maybe she would cut him some slack for the day they met. For the outburst she'd witnessed at the SAR Training Center. For the way he'd left without even saying goodbye.

He had been nothing but a gentleman to her on that drive. A wounded hero, according to Will. She'd only agreed to drive Dakota because she'd thought she'd never see him again. But here he was. Running down a mountain, helping her find two lost boys.

He couldn't be all bad.

Truth was, she didn't think he was bad in the first place. And that was the problem. She could all too easily see the good in him.

Dakota might be a good guy.

But *she* wouldn't be good for him.

Scout stopped. He sniffed again in a zigzag pattern until he found the scent cone swinging off to the right. He barked as they approached a cave hidden in the side of the slope.

"Scout, stay." Allie called into the darkness, "Ethan? Nolan? It's Allie."

She walked into the pitch black until she could hear whispers. "Remember me from this morning?"

"Allie?" A trembling voice echoed off the rock wall.

The cave narrowed enough that Allie could touch both sides of it, but the farther she walked in, the more the shadows took over. She called for Scout to join her. Thankfully, this time he came immediately and stuck by her.

"Yeah, it's me. I have Scout with me. And a friend. His name is Dakota. He's a firefighter." Little boys loved hero firemen, right?

She took a few steps before a swath of light cut through the black and lit her path. There, in the beam of Dakota's flashlight, the brothers sat huddled together against a stone, the older one holding the younger. Their faces were covered in dirt, with streaks from tears or sweat—probably both. Scout trotted over and barked. He licked Nolan's cheek.

"Good boy, Scout." Seeing the boys safe and relatively unharmed loosened her tight lungs. She needed to reward Scout for his hard work. But first she needed to make sure the boys were okay with Dakota.

"You guys sure scared us. Are you all right?" She approached them one tiny step at a time.

Ethan nodded and wiped his cheeks. "You found us. I told Nolan you could. That you were a nice lady and Scout would remember us."

"You were right. Scout found you." She crouched, assessing the brothers. "But we need to get you back. Your mom and dad are worried."

"He's not my dad!"

Allie froze. The last vestiges of fear in Ethan's eyes had seemed to morph to fury.

"I'm sorry. I didn't know." She winced. "Your mom, though, is really scared. We should get you back—"

But Ethan vehemently shook his head. "No. We can stay here. I have enough food. We're fine." He sniffed and lifted a strong chin in a surprising show of defiance. "I'm not going back."

Nolan cried though. His whole body shuddered. "I don't wanna see the bad man again. He'll kill us."

"Whoa, whoa, whoa. What bad man?" Dakota came closer to the boys.

Ethan stood quickly and moved in front of his brother. He held his own wrist, as though he might've injured it. "Who are you?"

"That's my friend Dakota. He came to help me find you. He's a firefighter."

Dakota held out a hand and gave the boys a friendly smile. It was a nice smile. Apparently Nolan thought so too. He jumped into Dakota's arms and wrapped his own chubby ones around Dakota's neck.

"Nolan!" Ethan yelled. "He's a stranger."

"It's okay, Ethan. Firemans are safe. And he's Allie's friend. Scout likes him too." Nolan gave his brother a wobbly grin.

Scout. Right. Allie pulled out Scout's absolute favorite toy, a now-stinky tugging rope. "Scout did such a good job finding you guys. I'm going to play with him now. Want to see?"

She dangled the rope in front of the Lab. Scout jumped and grabbed it with his mouth. He pulled, letting out a playful growl. Allie held tight. "Good boy!"

Both boys' eyes lit. Ethan stood a little straighter. Even Dakota seemed to soften, watching Scout play.

She held the toy out for Ethan to hold. "Wanna give it a try?" Maybe if he felt a little more in control of the situation, a little safer with them, she could convince them to leave. They still didn't have a lot of time.

Ethan held the rope with one hand. Scout tugged and immediately got the rope away from the boy.

"Try holding the rope with both hands." Allie snagged it from Scout and handed it back to Ethan.

"I can't. I hurt my hand."

Dakota approached, still holding Nolan in one arm. "Can I see? I took classes on first aid. I might even have a bandage we can use."

Ethan hesitated but eventually nodded. "Look over Nolan's leg first. He cut it when we fell."

Allie continued Scout's tug-of-war while she watched Dakota examine the boys.

Dakota glanced up. "I think Scout needs a new tugging rope. That one looks well-loved."

"That's for a reason. This toy is special. I only use this rope to reward Scout when he's done his job."

He grinned down at Nolan. "I think he did his job. He found you guys. I say give him all the stinky ropes he wants."

Nolan giggled.

Allie couldn't help but smile. "He did do a great job."

"So, do you only play with him or pet him as a reward?" Dakota said it with a sincere look on his face, a simple question. But accusation still burned within her.

"I…no. I'm still learning how to interact with Scout. It hasn't been as easy for me as it was with Dixie."

"I'm sure it's hard after losing her so suddenly. Especially when you were so close to her." There was no judgment in his tone, just simple understanding. Empathy.

Maybe she *had* been holding back with Scout. Belle had mentioned it too. She needed to change that. She sat down and really sank her fingers deep into his fur, massaging his flanks. "Good boy," she murmured into his floppy ear while they watched the others. Scout lay by her and rested his head on her lap.

Dakota pulled out a kit from his pack. Nolan winced when he poured water over a deep cut on his lower leg, but he didn't cry out.

"You cut this one good, little man. But not as good as me." Dakota lifted the leg of his Nomex pants and showed them a long, jagged scar that wrapped around his calf.

The boys gaped as if in awe. "What did you do?" Nolan asked.

"I fell off my bike. It took thirty-two stitches to get me back together." He puffed out his chest as if it were something to be proud of.

"Will I need stitches?" Nolan asked.

"You might. But if you do, you won't need thirty of them. I'll bandage it up for now to keep it clean and see what the doctor says when we get back. Deal?"

"Okay."

Dakota gently applied the gauze and taped it around Nolan's leg. "Now, let's look at your hand, Ethan. Where does it hurt?"

Ethan kept as much distance as he could but allowed Dakota to check his injury. He was definitely more cautious. And the way he'd become so angry when she'd mistakenly called Ray his dad made her wonder.

She nodded at Dakota, gesturing to the side of the cave.

"Hold your arm against your chest, just like this, while Allie helps me find something in my pack," he told Ethan. Stepping around the boy, he dropped his pack at Allie's feet.

"Do you think Ray is the 'bad man' they're scared of?" she whispered. "Jen definitely fit the mark of a woman in an abusive relationship."

"I wondered that too. It would explain her skittishness. And why Ethan doesn't want to go back."

"Yeah, I mean, she was obviously worried about the boys, but she cowered when Ray put his arm around her earlier. If that is the case, no wonder Ethan was slow in trusting you to look at his arm."

"Can't blame the kid if that Ray is the bad guy they're talking about." Dakota's jaw twitched, like he was clenching his teeth tight. He glanced over at the boys, a fierceness in his eyes that looked a lot like protectiveness.

He dug through his pack, keeping his voice low. "But we have to get out of this cave. Soon. The fire is heading right for us."

"We need to convince Ethan it's safe to leave."

"Agreed." Dakota went back to Ethan. "Let's get that arm stabilized." Scout wandered over to the guys and lay at Dakota's feet while he wrapped Ethan's arm in a makeshift sling with his bandana.

"Now that we have you two set, we need to get you back to the campground and probably a doctor." Allie picked up Scout's rope and stashed it away again.

"I don't wanna see the bad man." Nolan buried his face in Dakota's neck.

"Hey, buddy. It's okay." Dakota touched the boy's head. "I'm gonna keep you safe."

"That's right. Dakota was a cop before he was a firefighter." Allie held Ethan's backpack out to him. She helped lift the strap over his injured arm and settle it over his shoulders.

"A cop? Did you kill any bad guys?" Nolan asked with wide eyes.

"I saw a lot of bad guys as a cop, and we helped put them in prison so they couldn't hurt other people. Allie and I will keep you safe too. Even if she wasn't a police officer." He winked.

"Are you sure? That man—the bad man—he has a

gun." Ethan looked up at Allie, widened his big blue eyes, and bit down on his lower lip.

"Which man?" Dakota asked.

Neither boy answered. They looked at each other. Ethan gave the slightest shake of his head to his brother. A plea to keep silent?

Allie kneeled by Ethan. "Dakota and I will protect you. But right now there's a fire coming. This cave isn't safe, so we need to get back to your mom, okay?"

Ethan studied Dakota standing there, holding his little brother close.

"All right." He finally nodded. "We'll go with you, but if that man comes—"

"We'll make sure you're safe." Dakota offered his hand.

Ethan shook it.

"I believe this belongs to you." Allie held out what she'd found in the woods to Nolan.

"My hat!"

She plopped it on his head, and they headed toward the entrance. Dakota insisted on continuing to carry Nolan. She wanted to offer to hold Ethan's hand, but she wasn't sure the boy would like that. Instead, she offered him an encouraging smile as they stepped out of the cave.

Sparks flew through the air. They climbed the ridge that hid the cave only to see a raging wall of fire eating up the forest floor and swallowing the stately evergreens whole on the next hill. It was heading right toward them.

Not good.

Dakota's breath caught at the sight of the terror headed for them. An onslaught of fiery flames clambered up the massive trees and slithered along the ground, maybe five hundred yards away. Even here, red-hot embers rained down on them, the blaze so close he could feel the heat.

The fire blocked off their access to the trail behind the ridge. Between the gray smoke hanging in the air and the hot wind pushing the fire along its path, they would have to move fast.

Dakota grabbed his radio and called in to his team, letting them know they'd found the boys.

Kane's voice crackled over the radio. "You better book it. Fire skirted around the campgrounds but has already engulfed the entrance to the hiking trails. You're going to have to find another way back. Head north, then you can swing west toward an old logging road or east toward the river."

"Copy that." His stomach clenched. "Keep your face covered as much as possible," Dakota told Nolan as he tucked him tight against his chest. "I'm not going to let you get hurt."

The boys might not be in a safe home—something he knew a little about, being a son of Buck Masterson—but now that Dakota was here, he would make sure they were safe and that nothing would harm them. Not even a raging wildfire.

He showed Ethan how to hold his shirt collar up over his nose. Allie did the same.

"Stay right on my side. We move together." Dakota set a brisk pace through the forest. Hopefully Allie and Ethan could keep up.

"Where are we going?" Allie asked.

"We have to go north, deeper into the forest, and west to hit the old logging road out of here."

Hopefully.

They jogged farther. Every time Dakota looked uphill, the fire was closer. They all coughed, choking on the thick smoke.

"Come on, guys. We gotta keep moving." Dakota worked hard to keep his voice steady.

"I can't breathe." Ethan's pace slowed.

"I know it's hard, but you're doing great. We can't stop." His eyes and throat burned too. Nolan whimpered against his shirt. Scout stayed between Ethan and Allie, encouraging them to keep going. "You got this, bud," Dakota called to Ethan.

Allie looked over at him, sweat and worry all over her face. "I can't breathe either." Her voice wheezed.

Scout circled her, ran ahead, and stopped.

"We'll get to fresh air as soon as we can. You can do this, Allie."

She nodded and continued moving downhill. Maybe it was wishful thinking, but the air seemed to clear a little.

"What's that?" She pointed into the distance.

Between the smoke and trees, a cedar-shake roof emerged. "A cabin? Way out here?" Dakota peered through the haze to get a better view. In a small clearing below them, protected by the ridge they were on, sat an old log cabin with a stone chimney. A pile of freshly cut wood surrounded an old stump, and a tiny, dry creek bed lay off to the side of it.

"I bet we're not on the public campgrounds anymore." Allie coughed.

Dakota scanned the little building. "If there's a cabin, there's gotta be a road."

"Maybe we should warn them first? Or maybe there's a vehicle we can borrow."

"Someone has been here recently. There's newly split wood." He pointed to it. But one look behind him showed the fire had reached the peak and was starting downhill toward them. "We have to keep going." Dakota transferred Nolan to Allie. "Take the boys, and I'll scope it out quickly and catch up. Follow the ridge off to the side of the cabin. It should lead to the road—and move as fast as you can!"

Dakota watched them only for a second. Long enough to see that Nolan wasn't too heavy for her. He climbed off the small ridge of rock, then picked his way over boulders and around ponderosa pines and Douglas firs until he reached the clearing. Finally, he crossed the creek bed and moved toward the cabin. The structure itself looked old—unpainted, logs a weathered gray. Dakota quickly jumped up to the front porch and pounded on the door.

"Hey, there's a fire. If anyone is home, you need to leave. Now!"

No answer. He checked the windows. Dusty curtains blocked his view. The doors didn't budge. Didn't seem like anyone was around at the moment. Maybe they'd obeyed the evacuation order.

A quick orbit around the cabin didn't reveal any vehicles.

A low rumble sounded from up on the ridge above. Fire chewed up the trees covering the incline and crawled toward him. There was still time, though not much. Dakota sprinted away toward the side of the cabin. He found the dirt road, not much more than a narrow track, leading away from the clearing.

He ran, Allie and the boys not far ahead of him.

With the burden of Nolan slowing Allie down, Dakota easily caught up to them. Scout led the pack, galloping full speed ahead.

A glance back showed the fire gaining on them.

"We gotta go faster." Dakota scooped up Ethan and jogged along Allie's side. They huffed as they ran down the rutted tracks of an old trail. It was barely a road but easier than slapping tree branches and jumping over roots and boulders. The stinging eyes and throat didn't help, but Dakota sprinted on.

"The trail forks. Which way do we go?" Allie asked.

"This way." It was away from the campground, but also going farther from the fire.

"How long has it been?" Allie huffed.

"Only ten or fifteen minutes since I caught up to you."

She stumbled to a stop and set Nolan on his feet. She bent over her knees, sucking in deep breaths.

"I just"—breath—"need"—breath—"a minute," her voice rasped.

Dakota set Ethan down too and grabbed water from his pack. "Quick, drink this, then we have to go."

He kept the boys from looking behind them, but Allie's eyes widened as she glanced back. She gulped her water and leaned closer to him.

"The fire is gaining. It's going to reach us before we—" She looked down at the boys and clamped her mouth shut.

"I know." He dropped his voice low. "We need a miracle."

Not that he had any right to ask for one. But he was different now. He'd done everything he could to keep Allie and the boys safe. He'd seen God come through in the most unlikely of circumstances. A fight with his own brother to bring him to the place of accepting the help he'd desperately needed. A ride from a complete stranger to get him where he'd needed to go. So why not now?

Faith wasn't a guarantee that God would do what Dakota thought best, but they'd need Him if they were going to save these boys.

So, we could really use some help right about now, Lord.

Allie finished her water but started coughing. She couldn't catch her breath. No way could she keep carrying Nolan and move as fast as they needed to.

Looking down at Ethan, Dakota laid a gentle hand on his shoulder. "Can you run?"

The boy nodded.

"Good." He held his hands out, and Nolan quickly jumped into his arms. "Come on, Allie. We have to go."

She coughed but nodded. Scout took off in a flash, running full speed ahead of them. They lost sight of him in the black smoke.

"Scout!" Allie yelled.

They sprinted after him. Behind them, the fire was a locomotive barreling toward them, torching the trees, flames exploding off the tops. Fire dripped down around them, igniting the pine needles lining their path.

Allie started to scream, even as she ran.

And inside, he was screaming too.

FOUR

HER LUNGS BURNED. HER EYES BURNED. HER muscles burned.

Allie was already on fire.

The panic in Dakota's eyes as he glanced behind them didn't help. The snapping and crackling of the fire surrounded them. Crashes of bigger trees falling sounded further away, but the flames were close, eating up the orange pine needles covering the forest floor.

Please, God. Save us. I know I have so much to still make up for. But these boys, they deserve to live.

Somehow, Allie found another burst of speed. Ahead of her, Ethan cried out and fell, and she nearly stumbled over him. They all stopped.

Dakota, already holding Nolan, grabbed Ethan by the arm. "C'mon, Ethan!" He rebalanced Nolan behind him.

Ethan crumbled back to the ground. "I can't!"

"Can you walk?" Allie asked the boy.

He shook his head, biting down on his lip—probably to hold back tears. A technique she knew well.

"I know, bud. But we can't cry. We have to run!"

"I'll carry him." Dakota knelt down.

Allie shook her head. "You already have—"

"We don't have time to argue. Just help him up so I can—"

A sound came through the forest, blaring, as if someone was leaning on their truck horn.

Yes! Behind them on the road, an ancient yellow Ford pickup came out of the smoke and raced toward them. A man with a shock of white-gray hair and a thick beard of the same color waved to them from the open window of the truck. "Get in the back! Hurry!"

Not waiting for introductions with this strange angel of mercy, Allie grabbed Nolan from Dakota and set him into the bed of the truck.

"Scout! Come!" Allie spun in a quick circle. "Scout?"

Dakota lifted Ethan into the back and then hopped up to join them.

"I can't find Scout." Allie peered through the smoke and ash.

Dakota held a hand out for her and pulled her into the truck bed. "We'll keep an eye out for him. He's probably right up ahead."

Allie sat against the cab. Her eyes watered as she wrapped her arms around Nolan, trying not to unravel.

Dakota gave a quick pound on the roof to signal they were set, and the truck took off.

Behind them, the fire raged on, barreling toward them. But the old truck rushed ahead and outran the flames. Within a few minutes, they were surrounded by green trees again. The air was clearer, and Allie could breathe again, even though her throat was scraped raw.

She moved to the side of the truck bed and craned her neck to scan the forest. The wind whipped her hair across her face.

"Scout! Scout! Here, boy," she called out, hoping her voice would carry over the fire and somehow Scout would find her. Dakota and Ethan called too. Mile after mile until they couldn't yell anymore. She fell back down against the cab once more.

Nolan cuddled up against her. "Where's Scout?"

Allie's own eyes filled with tears. She smoothed the sweaty hair off his forehead. His round cheeks were covered in dirt and ash. But she couldn't open her mouth to say anything.

Dakota leaned over to be heard over the wind. "Scout's a smart dog. He probably found an even faster way away from the fire. He'll be okay."

Nolan nodded, but tears cut down his face. "I liked Scout." He leaned back against Allie.

For a moment, Allie allowed herself the small luxury of relishing his presence. A little boy snug in her arms. He was younger than—

No. She couldn't go there.

Dakota leaned toward her. "Hey, we made it. We're okay."

She bit down on her lip and nodded. "Yeah. We did. But…Scout." Her voice cracked. "Belle was right."

"About what?"

"I kept Scout at a distance. I should've tried harder. Done better with him. I can't really blame him for running off—"

"No way. We're gonna find Scout. He's got amazing instincts. He's gonna survive."

"Well, I'm not leaving until I find him."

He gave her shoulder a light squeeze. "I'll help you look."

After bouncing down the rutted dirt track, the truck turned onto a more level gravel road and eventually wound its way to the highway. Before turning onto the paved road, they stopped.

The older man in his red flannel shirt and pants stained with ash and soot came around to the back of the truck. He wore suspenders and work boots, almost like a lumberjack version of Santa Claus. "Where you folks need to go?"

"The campground—"

"The hospital." Dakota spoke over her. "You and the boys need to get checked out first. I'll tell the parents to meet us at the hospital."

He was right. Jen would be worried sick. But with their injuries, it was a good call.

Allie turned to the stranger. "Would you mind?"

"Not at all. I can't stick around, but I certainly don't mind dropping you off."

"I'm Allie. This is Dakota." She motioned to the boys. "Nolan and Ethan."

"Nice to meet you folks. I'm Henry."

"Did you happen to see a black Lab? My dog was with us, but he ran ahead, and we lost him."

"I didn't, but I'll be sure to keep an eye out for him." With a quick nod, he was back in the truck, and they were on their way to Ember.

Dakota radioed his team, and Allie called Jen, telling her to meet them at the hospital. Afterward, she passed a water bottle and protein bar to the boys.

Nolan eagerly ate and within minutes, fell asleep against her.

Dakota chugged his water but took his time with the bar. "Thanks."

She gave him a weak smile. "I should be thanking you. Not that a smashed bar and some tepid water is much of an appreciation gift. The boys and I never would've made it out of that forest without you."

Dakota shrugged as if saving people's lives was no biggie. Then he turned to Ethan.

"Ethan, who is the scary man you said you saw on the trail?"

The boy stuffed another bite of his bar into his mouth. The wind blew through his sweaty blond hair, and his blue eyes narrowed. He looked from Allie to Dakota, almost as if assessing them.

"We want to help you," Allie urged him with smile. "Dakota was a police officer, remember? And I work with law enforcement all the time. I search for lost people."

Ethan released a shaky breath. "Last time we were camping, Nolan and I went for a hike. I was looking for a blue grouse for my Boy Scout badge, so we went off the trail even though my mom told me not to. We walked for a long time. Then we heard guys shouting. We hid. We were by that cabin you found, because I remembered that funny roof. And this man—" Ethan swallowed hard. His eyes welled with tears.

Dakota stilled. "What did he do?"

"The other man…the one with a necklace…he tried to walk away, but the tall man with the ponytail shot him in the back. He fell down, and then he shot him in the head too."

For real? They'd seen a *murder*?

No wonder the boys were scared. But maybe a combination of fear and strong imaginations had conjured up this story. They could've seen something else and misinterpreted it.

"Why did you want to go back today?" Allie asked him.

"We weren't trying to go back. We were trying to run away."

"Why did you want to run away?" Dakota asked softly.

Ethan clamped his mouth shut. Clearly, he was done talking.

She was about to ask more when she caught the subtle shake of Dakota's head. Maybe being a guy, he understood better when to push and when to wait. She'd trust him…for now.

They bumped along in the rusty truck bed to the hospital. Vehicles filled the parking lot, but the old man pulled up right out front.

Allie stood on shaky legs and lifted Nolan out of the truck while Dakota helped Ethan. She turned to Henry. "Thanks for—"

The engine revved, and he was gone.

"Who was that guy?" Allie looked at Dakota.

"No clue. But I wish I could've at least shaken his hand and thanked him for saving us."

They walked into the hospital. Locals covered in soot and ash, some of them bleeding, milled around the ER lobby. And standing among them, Jen and her husband Ray. They were talking with a man in a tan deputy uniform.

"Nolan! Ethan!" Jen rushed to engulf both boys in her arms.

"Mommy!" Nolan launched himself at her, and his

arms clenched around her neck. She scooped him up, crying.

Ethan was limping, holding on to Dakota's arm for support. When Ray walked over to them, Ethan stiffened.

"We need these boys seen now. You can go." Ray wrapped an arm around Jen, who'd gotten up and lifted Nolan with her. She walked over to Ethan and pulled him against her hip in a hug.

"Let's go." Ray moved them toward the counter.

Ethan hopped on one foot. Ray tried to offer him an arm, but the boy shook his head. "I can do it myself."

The four of them were quickly ushered back by a nurse.

A muscle in Dakota's jaw twitched like he was clenching his teeth.

So he'd noticed it too.

"Do you think Ray is the scary man the boys were talking about?" Allie whispered. "Or do you think Ethan was telling the truth about the men in the woods? With a gun?"

"I don't know. But they aren't comfortable around him, even if he isn't the ponytailed killer."

She shuddered. "Is there really a body in the woods—one that's been out there for weeks?"

Dakota spun to face her. "I can't leave the boys here with Ray if he's dangerous."

Allie fiddled with the hanging straps from her pack, her gaze going from Dakota back to the ER. "But beyond kidnapping them, what do we do? And Scout. I have to go find him." Her throat squeezed.

"Scout will be okay. But you should get that

cough checked out." Dakota's frown pinched his brow together.

Did he know something she didn't? "What is it?"

Dakota dropped his voice. "We can't get back there with the patients unless one of us is a patient too."

Oh! "Right."

Allie coughed and approached the desk. If she was honest, she probably did need to be checked out.

After a little paperwork, a nurse ushered her and Dakota into the small emergency department. She checked her vitals. "Might as well settle in for a bit. With all the other fire-related injuries, we're short-staffed, and it might be a while." She turned on the television that hung in the corner of the room and handed the remote to Allie. "Let me know if you need anything else."

As soon as she left, Allie hopped off the bed. "I'm going to see if I can find Jen and talk to her alone."

"I'll go—"

"You should stay here." She stopped Dakota with a hand to his chest. His very muscular chest. Over the last few hours, she'd seen a lot of different sides of Dakota Masterson. He really was a hero.

Don't get carried away, Allie!

She dropped her hand. "Last thing we need is you getting into another public brawl."

Dakota snapped his mouth closed. Hurt flashed in his eyes.

Aw, why had she said *that*?

She winced. "Sorry. I just mean...it's just that you're rather...intimidating. If Jen will speak to anyone, it will be me."

"Fine."

Obviously Dakota wasn't happy about it, but he stayed.

Allie slipped out of the tiny partition behind the curtain and heard familiar voices across the hall. The door was cracked open. Ray was nowhere to be seen, but Jen spoke with the doctor as he examined the cut on Nolan's leg. Ethan sat in one chair with his leg propped up on another.

"I'll have Ethan sent down to X-ray, and the nurses will prep Nolan for some stitches. I'll be back when we get those records," a voice said, probably the doctor.

Allie leaned against the wall and pretended to look at her phone when the man in scrubs and a white lab coat came out of the room. As soon as he turned the corner to the nurse's station, Allie went in.

"Hey, just wanted to check on everyone." She offered Jen a warm smile. "Are you holding up okay?"

Jen nodded and held Nolan's hand. "I am now." She smoothed the boy's blond hair off his forehead.

"Great. Um…could I talk to you a sec, in the hall?"

Her gaze flicked to the doorway. "The doctor is coming right—"

"It won't take long. I promise. And we'll be in the hall."

Jen followed her to the corridor. Her gaze shifted around, like she was on the lookout and would bolt at any second. A woman used to living on edge, watching for a threat.

"Jen, are you safe?"

"What?" She finally looked at Allie. "I don't know

what—" Her hand fluttered around her throat. Jen wrapped her other arm around herself.

Allie lowered her voice. "Are you safe. In your home. With Ray?"

"I'm fine." She smiled a little too brightly. "Really."

Fine? Then why were her hands trembling? "Are you? Because the boys told us—"

"Boys tell stories." Her voice came out forcefully. "Like I told you before, they make stuff up. You can't listen—"

"I think it's more than that. You can tell me the truth. We can get help for you if you need it."

Jen shook her head and glanced down the hall. "No need. I'm fine. Great, even. The boys are…fine. Well, they will be once the doc sees them. But they'll be okay."

Allie didn't believe her, but without proof or Jen's cooperation, her hands were tied. Ray's voice carried from farther down the hall. She was running out of time.

"You have my number, right?" Allie whispered.

Jen looked at her and nodded.

"Okay. Then you call me. Anytime. For anything. Understand? I will be there as fast as I can."

Ray and a nurse came around the corner. Jen glanced at them and then lifted her chin as she faced Allie. "Thanks again for finding them." She slipped back into the exam room.

Ray glowered as he approached. "What are you doing?"

"Just wanted to see how the boys are." Allie gave him a fake smile and walked across the hall to her own partition.

"Well?" Dakota asked. He sat in a chair, leg bouncing as if he was ready to spring into action.

Allie shook her head. "She won't admit anything is going on, but I know the signs. She's scared. I made sure she had my number, but I don't think we can do much else except report what they said."

"That's not good enough." Dakota stood. "Men like that don't deserve to go free." He turned and stalked out of the room.

And she had the distinct feeling he wasn't only talking about Ray.

Dakota walked back out to the lobby. He'd heard what Jen had said. Ethan might be making up stories about a bad man shooting someone, but he hadn't even thought of that while the boys told their story. They'd been so adamant, and there was usually a grain of truth in any story. He'd learned that as a cop.

Something told him the real reason the boys had wanted to run away…

Was Ray.

Dakota knew exactly what those boys were going through. This time he was going to do something about it.

"Wait. Dakota." Allie grabbed his arm. For a woman small in stature, she was strong. "What do you mean, 'men like that'?"

He stopped before reaching the lobby and faced her.

"I mean men like my old man." Buck Masterson had known how to avoid leaving marks that would be seen on Dakota's body, but it was the wounds inside that took much longer to heal.

"What did he do?"

Things a sweet woman like Allie shouldn't have to hear, but if it helped her understand the real danger those boys were in…"Let's just say I was a convenient target for his rage. And as sheriff of a large county in the middle of nowhere, he knew how to throw his weight around and not get caught."

Allie's eyes widened. "What about your mom?"

"My mom?" He tried really hard to shrug like it wasn't excruciating to remember. "She tried to smooth things over. She blamed the liquor, or my behavior. But eventually she got tired of being knocked around too, and we left."

"So you got away? She's okay now?"

"Okay? No. She never recovered." Bitterness had taken root, and she'd found escape. "I tried. I tried so hard to take care of her. But…in the end it didn't matter. She had her own addictions."

Allie's small hand latched onto his forearm. "What happened?" Her voice, only a quiet whisper, somehow wound through him and found the aching wounds inside. Places he'd never shown anyone.

"A meth overdose." He swallowed hard, the picture of his mom's gaunt figure on the tattered green couch as clear as if it had been yesterday. One moment she'd been high, spouting things she'd hidden from him his whole life. And then she was gone. "Right before she died, though, she told me I had a brother."

"Wait. You didn't know about Will?"

He jammed his hands in his pockets. "She'd never told me. Buck had never said a thing about having another son. For a moment I had this glimmer of hope. I had a brother out there somewhere. Maybe I wasn't so alone, but my mom…she looked at me—"

Thinks he's better than us. Thinks we're trash. So don't go looking for him or anything.

"And what?"

"She told me Will hated us. That he thought he was better than us and wanted nothing to do with me because he was some big-time federal agent. For a long time I believed her. Later I found out Will never even knew I existed. But this is what I *do* know. Those two brothers deserve better than what Will and I have been through. From both parents."

He charged over to the deputy, who was chatting with the older woman behind the counter. When they broke off their conversation, he said, "Deputy, do you know the family that went back there with the two young boys?"

"The Haroldsons? Yeah, I know them. Why do you ask?" The man stared down at him, frowned a little.

"I just want to make sure those boys are safe. They were pretty scared and talked about a scary man and wanting to get away from him. Any chance that could be the stepfather?"

"I'm sure the boys are fine." He turned back to the woman.

"So you've never had any domestic complaints or calls to their place?"

The deputy faced Dakota again, this time with a sigh. "I don't know who you are—"

"I'm Dakota Masterson. I'm with—" It was on the tip of his tongue to say *with the Benson PD SWAT*. But that wasn't true anymore. "Jude County Hotshots."

"Well, Hotshot, I appreciate you finding those boys and saving them, I truly do. But you've got no other say here in what happens. You're not a cop or a deputy in this town. So unless you have some hard evidence, you better not start making accusations against a local."

Really? "I might be a hotshot now, but I'm former SWAT, so I know the drill. It's pretty obvious the boys aren't comfortable around Ray. You saw how Ethan reacted to him."

"Yeah. Pretty much how I reacted toward my stepdad too when he first showed up." The deputy took his glare down a notch and stepped away from the counter. "Truth is, Ray Haroldson might not be my favorite person, but he *is* their stepfather. Not much I can do about that."

"Darn right you can't!" Ray stomped over toward them. "You got something to say, Fireman, you say it to my face."

He shouldn't, but Dakota was itching for a fight. To put a jerk like Ray in his place. Maybe he could goad Ray into admitting something so the deputy could charge him. "All right, tell me, do you get your kicks out of hurting innocent children? Ever slap your wife around? Just for the fun of it?"

Ray sneered but didn't come closer. His voice was a mean growl. "You don't know nothin'."

"Yeah? That's why the boys told *me* they saw a man shot to death." Dakota faced him down. "You know anything about that?"

"About two kids telling stories 'cause they watch too many action movies?" Ray squared up on Dakota.

The deputy moved toward them. "Hold up, you two. Step back. No need to—"

Dakota didn't dare break eye contact with Ray. "I know if you hurt those boys, you're going to regret it."

"Is that a threat?" Ray got right up in Dakota's face, his chest bumping into him.

And that was it.

Dakota shoved him back and let a right cross loose. Ray had better reflexes than he'd figured. His head swung back, Dakota's fist merely glancing off his jaw. But it was on.

Ray charged at him. Chairs screeched as they slid across linoleum. Dakota blocked the hit and jabbed, catching Ray in the soft flesh of his midsection, right under the ribs.

Before he could send his left hook, the deputy leaped in and pulled Dakota off.

"Cut it out! The both of you."

Dakota pushed against the deputy's hold on him, but the guy had an iron grip.

Ray staggered back and fell. He wiped off blood trickling from the corner of his mouth. "Did you see what he did? You arrest this man!"

"I should throw *both* of you in the holding cell. Get up. And go check on the boys." The deputy released Dakota and stepped in between the men. "Go on, now, Haroldson."

Ray stood and pointed at Dakota. "You better stay clear of my family, you hear?"

"I mean it, Ray," the deputy said. "Get out of here before I throw you in jail for disorderly conduct." The deputy waited until Ray left the room. He swung around to face Dakota. "And you, you don't have any authority or jurisdiction. Stay out of it."

Dakota fumed. "You're just going to let him go? Don't you care about those boys?"

"Ray is a mean cuss, but there are laws. And *you* are not authorized to enforce them. That's my job. You better stay out of it, because beating the man senseless might feel good for a moment—and don't think I haven't dreamed of doing it myself—but I'll still be hauling you in for assault if you do, and that won't help those boys none. Got it?"

So the man did suspect something, but he had to play it carefully. While the rage dissipated, Dakota caught his breath. He looked around the waiting room. Chairs were knocked over and scattered. An elderly lady with a cane sat wide-eyed in the corner.

And right by the door that led to the emergency department stood Allie.

Great. Just when she was starting to trust him enough to see him as something more than a violent man, she'd witnessed this. The accusation in her face said it all.

To her, he would only ever be a broken man with a temper.

FIVE

Allie sat on the hot curb next to Dakota in front of the hospital. She wasn't a firefighter like Emily. She had no clue how to douse the fire raging in the man next to her. The heat radiated off his body as the sun baked them both. An older woman with obviously dyed black hair and a bright green top with huge purple flowers walked past with the man that must love her—or at least love her enough to wear a polo in the same obnoxious green. Allie tried to ignore the woman's obvious stare. The paper sack with her prescription cough medicine gave her something to hold at least. She twisted the bag, unsure how to bring up what'd just happened.

The last time Allie had seen Dakota using his fists like that, it had been his own brother on the other end of it. She'd been horrified. But this time...well, this time it was completely different. She'd almost cheered when Dakota had got that last punch in before the deputy pulled the men apart. Too bad the cop hadn't thrown Ray in jail then and there. Instead, the deputy had sent Ray right back to his family.

He may have tried to keep his voice low, but on

her way back to her exam room, she'd heard the threats he'd muttered to Jen.

What have you been telling people?

Nothing, Ray. I swear.

If I hear anything—

You won't. The boys are sorry. They…just got lost, is all.

You better keep them in line, or else they'll be in a lot more—

Of course, the nurse had come around the corner then and called Allie back to her own room.

When she'd finished with the nurse practitioner, she'd tried to talk to Dakota about it. He wouldn't look her in the eye, but he did manage to release his clenched jaw enough to say, "Emily is on her way to pick us up." Then he'd walked out here and sat under the blazing sun, lost in his own thoughts. He hadn't said a word since. And Allie didn't know how to break the silence between them.

One thing was sure. There was a lot more to this man than she'd ever realized. Maybe she could start there.

"Kota, the way you stood up for those boys—" It made her wish she'd waited for someone like that. Someone who protected others and didn't run away at the first sign of trouble, casting her or anyone else in their way aside. "It was—"

Dakota stood and walked a few steps away. "It was useless."

"No, it wasn't. You barely know these boys, but you stood up for them. And the way you carried them through the burning forest…" Well, whatever he'd been in the past, he'd been quite the hero today. "I just want to say I'm sorry I didn't believe you at first about changing."

"Probably haven't." He shook his head, his mouth set in a firm line, jaw clenched tight and pulsing, like he was grinding his molars.

Just as Allie was going to say more, his intense blue stare narrowed in on her. "The team doesn't know." He released a long, slow breath like he'd just gotten something huge off his chest.

"What?" Allie tried to make sense of what was obviously a big deal to him.

"The hotshots. They know I was a cop. Well, some of them. Maybe. But…they don't know about the rest. About rehab."

Oh. That. "Why are you trying to hide it?"

"I'm not. But…I have a lot to prove here. If they knew I'm an addict—"

"Dakota, you went to rehab. It's nothing to be ashamed of."

"Maybe. But I don't want to be defined by it. It's bad enough everyone I knew back in Benson looks at me with judgment. I let down my team there. But I have another chance here. Understand?"

Oh, she could understand all right. The judgment. The guilt and shame. For a moment, she was back at that place—

His warm hand grabbed hers, pulling her out of the memory before it could suck her under. "And I'm not asking you to lie. It's just…could you keep my history, about rehab and getting kicked off the SWAT team, between us?"

"I…"

"They need to know they can trust me to do the job I have now. I can't mess this up. It's all I've got."

"That's not true, Kota. You have family and friends. And who cares about what happened back in

Benson? You're a hero. You saved those boys. You saved me. That's who you are. You're not the troublemaker you claimed to be when I first met you."

"Well, it's not like I was going to leave you there in a burning forest with two boys alone. Of course I would do everything in my power to keep you safe."

He didn't know how rare that was. "Not everyone is like that." Some men showed up with all the big romantic gestures, luring naive women into a fantasy world. And the minute the fantasy bubble popped, they left her high and dry to face all the consequences alone.

Maybe Dakota was different. It seemed like he was a really good guy. Sure, he had a temper. He was passionate. But his passion was protecting others. Not trying to get ahead or take advantage of the innocent. He deserved his fresh start.

Before she could say anything, Emily pulled up in her 4Runner. "Anybody need a ride?"

Dakota held the front door for Allie, then threw their packs into the trunk and climbed in the back seat.

"You two sure had an exciting day. But no rest for the weary. The fire is out of control, and they need us on the line as soon as we can, Masterson." Emily glanced at him in the rearview mirror.

"Sure, but what will you do now, Allie?" he asked her.

"I'm not leaving Ember. I don't care what that deputy says. Jen and the boys need help."

"Maybe you should go home. I'll watch out for the boys," Dakota said from the backseat. "It's dangerous out here. For you too."

"But you'll be out fighting fires. Someone needs to

stick close by for Jen and Ethan and Nolan. And I have to find Scout. He's out there somewhere. I can't leave him behind," Allie said.

"You can stay with us at the firebase," Emily offered. "It might be a little cramped with the extra crews coming in, but you can stay in the ladies' bunk room or with me and Sanchez and Jojo at our rental house in town."

Allie glanced at Dakota. Did he want her to stay? Not that it mattered. She couldn't leave now. "If you're sure you don't mind, yeah, I'll stay at your place."

They pulled into the vacant campground. It was eerily silent as they stepped out of the car. One of the crew fire trucks was still there. Emily and Dakota walked over and talked with some of the team. Allie threw her backpack into her own SUV. Opening up the back, she saw Scout's kennel and blanket. She fingered the well-worn piece of fleece, tears immediately stinging her eyes.

Scout. She couldn't even keep even a dog safe.

Her phone buzzed in her pocket. Belle. She wiped her cheeks before answering.

"Hey, you must've made it home, huh?" Allie sank onto her truck and watched the hotshot crew. Dakota and Emily stood over one of the picnic tables. Dakota's whole body leaned in to study the map, intense concentration on his face.

"Yeah, I'm back home. So, how did the training go. How's Scout?"

"Well—" Allie swallowed hard. "Not so great." She told Belle what'd happened.

"You were caught in that forest fire? Allie, what were you thinking, walking into a wildfire?"

"I was thinking I couldn't leave those two boys lost in the forest. What was I supposed to do? Leave them to die?"

"Obviously not, but—" Belle paused. "Now that they're safe, why don't you leave? You could be here by tonight. We could still have these next four days together."

Allie shoved off the vehicle. "Leave? Scout is out here somewhere. Lost. You expect me to abandon him? I won't!"

"Take it easy, Al. I forgot about Scout. It was just a suggestion."

"Well, it was a bad one."

"I'm just...I'm worried about you. Your voice sounds awful. You probably have smoke inhalation. You need to be careful and take care of yourself." Belle's concern helped calm some of the ire, but it didn't change the facts.

"I can't leave my dog lost in the woods. I'm staying until I find him." Allie stuffed her free hand deep into her pocket. She might not deserve another chance, not after all she'd done. But she wouldn't leave until she'd exhausted every resource. Because maybe Dakota wasn't the only one with a second chance here. Maybe this was a test. A test to see how much she was willing to do to make up for her past mistakes.

It was a test she intended to pass this time.

Finally, Dakota was doing what he'd come to Montana to do: fight fires.

The crew moved in a line around trees, rocks, and

brush. Kane worked next to him, sawing down vegetation to stop the fire from spreading toward a small community of homes nestled in one of the mountain valleys. One of the guys up the line blared Metallica on a small speaker. Hammer called for his brother Mack to throw him a water, which he caught easily. Dakota's chain saw buzzed and spat sawdust into the air as he cut into the trunk of a beautiful spruce. A sad but necessary sacrifice. He moved on to the next tree.

On the outside, he was pure hotshot. Part of a team again.

Inside?

The cop instinct in him wouldn't die. And it was an instinct that might get him into trouble.

He wanted to snatch Ethan and Nolan out of Ray's grasp and find a safe place for them. And while one part of him regretted coming to blows, the other part hadn't got in nearly enough to satisfy the burning rage against the injustice of it all.

With one last slice of the chain saw, Dakota felled a scrubby tree. He killed the saw, hefted the skinny trunk, and pitched it over the break line.

"You got some anger there you're trying to quench?"

Huh. Kane talking? That was new. Usually he just sat around listening, rarely joining in the conversations and banter in their short breaks.

"Maybe."

"This about those lost boys and their stepfather?"

"You heard about that?"

"Heard you got into a fistfight."

Wonderful. Who else knew? Hopefully it didn't get back to Commander Dafoe. Dakota still had a lot of money to pay back to his brother, and the sign-on bonus he was counting on to do that was only good after three months. Not to mention, with Emily Micah here and Allie and her connections in Benson, Will would definitely hear if Dakota got kicked off the team.

"Who did you hear it from?"

Kane shrugged and killed his own chain saw. He picked up the big branches and shrubs he'd cut and threw them out of the way. "Doesn't matter. I'm guessing you had your reasons."

"I did. Innocent children shouldn't be subjected to living with a man like that. Those boys are in danger."

"You think the stepdad is beating up on them?"

Dakota hefted another heavy limb, but it barely budged. "I don't have proof, but yeah. I do. I don't get how Jen can stay with someone like that."

Houston James came and helped lift the fallen pine. "A lot of people in those situations think that's what they deserve. They don't really believe that there's anything better. She may even come from an abusive situation herself, where it seems normal."

"How do you know all this?" Dakota grunted as they carried the log across the break line.

"I'm a youth pastor. Well, I *was* a youth pastor. You see a lot working with teens. A lot of brokenness." Houston nodded and together they dropped their load.

Dakota picked up a branch light enough to throw this time. He pitched it to the other side. "Yeah, but Jen is a grown woman. She can leave. She can report Ray. But she's choosing to stay. Staying at the expense of her own children."

Okay. He'd done enough therapy in rehab to

admit it might be harder to empathize with her with all the history he had with his own mother. He'd *been* Ethan and Nolan. But even his own mother had eventually left. Did Jen have any idea what staying was doing to her sons?

Did she even care?

"Did the boys say anything to you?" Houston asked.

"They might've made up some story of seeing a bad man get shot in the forest, but I think that's just a cover up."

Kane stopped. "They said they saw someone out here get shot?"

"Yeah, but I think it was all made-up." Dakota mopped the sweat off his forehead with his bandanna.

Houston stilled too. "What exactly did the kids say?"

Dakota played back the conversation with Ethan. "He said they went off-trail and saw a man with a ponytail shoot a guy in the back and then the head. They mentioned a necklace too."

"The man was shot in the back *and* in the head?" Kane came closer, his voice low.

"Yeah. What of it? Why are you acting so weird?" Dakota sat on one of the stumps.

Houston sank down next to him. "The body Sophie and I found burned to a crisp? In an area that hadn't been reached by the fire yet? It wasn't too far from the campground hiking trails. No identification last I heard, but COD was a gunshot to the back and the head. And a necklace was found near the body."

A chill cut through Dakota. Kane shoved his shoulder. "No surprise you didn't connect the two, since you were distracted by a certain search and rescue handler."

"Knock it off." The last thing he needed was the hotshots asking questions about how he knew Allie. She'd never said if she would keep the old Dakota where he was. In the past. And now she was staying with Emily, Sanchez, and Jojo. Hopefully it wouldn't come up. But the boys—

"You really think those boys witnessed *that* murder?" Dakota asked. "That body was nowhere near a cabin. That's where the boys saw everything go down."

"The body had been moved. Someone tried to cover it up. Did the boys say when they saw the shooting?"

Dakota shook his head. "Ethan just said the last time they were here. I don't know when that was."

"Sophie and I found the body when we were out looking for her horses after the evacuation for the ranch came through. We brought the body back to town, but I haven't heard anything since. She thought the guy was her brother, dead. But it turned out he's alive." Houston grabbed his canteen and took a long drink. He grabbed his chain saw and joined the others on the saw crew.

Dakota pinched the bridge of his nose. He'd been so focused on keeping his past a secret and doing his job that he hadn't connected the boys' story with the body Houston had found. "Did they figure out who did it?" he asked Kane.

Kane shrugged. "No idea. Guess the only way to know what actually happened to the guy is to talk to the kids again."

He snatched another branch off the ground to

drag it over the line. "That's a little tricky since I'm not a cop."

"But you were."

Dakota stilled. He'd never said so. And Kane wasn't asking. He knew. "Not anymore. Besides, pretty sure after I let fists fly with Ray Haroldson, I've burned any chance of the LEOs sharing info with me." He squared off with Kane. "But you seem to know more about this body than I do. Did they identify it yet?"

Kane shrugged. "Dunno. I imagine you still have friends in law enforcement. Ask them."

Thankfully, he let it drop, and they got back to work. If he wanted to get into Dakota's sordid past, Dakota had some questions of his own he was pretty sure Kane wouldn't want to answer. There was some kind of history with Sanchez, Kane, Hammer, and Saxon. Maybe even Ham's little brother Mack was in on it, but they were all rather secretive. They came across like a military unit, guys who moved in sync. Who seemed hyperaware of the world around them.

Who reacted faster than Dakota had on SWAT.

"How about you?" Dakota eased into the question, all casual-like. "Who were you before Ember?"

Kane only snorted under his breath.

He wasn't going to answer? Dakota didn't have time to dig when there was more going on in this forest than just a raging wildfire.

It could involve a murder, if the boys were to be believed.

But was Dakota projecting his history onto Ethan when he assumed Ray was abusive and the story of the bad man was a cry for help? Had the brothers really witnessed a murder? Allie had seemed to think they were scared of Ray as well, so at least that was confirmed.

If the wrong person found out Ethan and Nolan were witnesses to a murder, they might be in even more danger than a simple jerk stepfather situation.

Kane continued clearing the brush they'd mowed down. "So, what's going on with that woman we saw this morning? Emily's friend."

"Allie? Nothing."

"But you know her, right?"

"Not well, but yeah. We met last year." *When she saw me lose it and then drove me eight hours to rehab.*

"So…there's no relationship or anything?"

"Wait a minute." Dakota spun around, frowning. "You wanna ask Allie out or something? What about Sanchez?"

"Sanchez?" Kane balked. "What are you talking about?"

Dakota raised an eyebrow. "You watch her. Like a hawk. All the time. I mean, she's got more attitude than I like, but if that's your thing—"

"It's not like that." Kane grabbed his saw and hiked uphill toward the next patch of vegetation. "And you have no idea what you're talking about."

Dakota followed after him. "Then how is it?"

"Not…that. And that's all I'm saying on the matter."

If this were his old SWAT team, Dakota would know how far was okay to push or tease or when to back off. But this *wasn't* his old team. This wasn't the group of guys he'd once considered as close as family. Gage still called. Liam had moved to a federal task force, and both Blake and Jasper were detectives in different departments.

They'd all tried to stay tight over the last year, but it wasn't the same. Benson SWAT wasn't working together day in and day out. After Dakota left, the whole team had disbanded anyway. They weren't putting their lives on the line to protect each other and the citizens of Benson. They might be cops still at least, but Dakota wasn't one of them anymore.

And there was no one but himself to blame for that.

"Let's get this break line done." Kane yanked on the rope start. His saw revved to life, the loud motor putting an end to the conversation.

Fine with Dakota. He started his own chain saw and sliced through the branches in their path. The others followed in line. Some on the saw crew, others with their Pulaski pick hoes and pick rakes, digging through the ground to clear a thick black line of soil.

Hopefully, removing all the fuel would stop the fire.

Dakota watched Kane as he attacked a thick lodgepole pine. Probably he shouldn't begrudge the guy if he wanted to ask Allie out.

After all, the woman was stunning, smart, and brave. She didn't back down from danger. He liked that spunk. The way she was tenacious going into a dangerous tinderbox of a forest to find the Haroldson boys wasn't something a guy found every day. When they'd all had to run, she'd fought the pain and pushed through.

Kane seemed like the decent sort too, but he didn't like to picture Kane and Allie together.

At all.

A tickle in the back of Dakota's throat demanded attention. He stopped his chain saw and dug in his pack for water. He couldn't afford to get distracted by thoughts of Allie.

Dakota needed to find out more about this dead guy. Maybe he should go into Ember and see if he could talk to the medical examiner. Find out who the man was. Then he'd find a way to talk to the boys—

"Watch out!"

A half-burnt Douglas fir some fifteen feet away swayed toward the line. Dakota jumped out of the way. He lifted his left arm to shield his face from the branches and sparks crashing toward him.

Pain seared his side as he fell to the rocky soil.

SIX

SHE HAD TO DO SOMETHING. ALLIE DRUMMED HER fingers on the now pristine counter and glanced around the Jude County Hotshots' base kitchen. The lemon-scented cleaner still lingered in the air. There had to be something more to do. But the stainless steel sink sparkled, the floors were swept and mopped, and no more science experiments sat rotting in the fridge. Instead, she had raw oatmeal chocolate chip cookies ready to slide into the oven when her main dish was done baking. She released a long sigh and checked the mac and cheese. According to Emily's recipe, it still needed time.

She'd rather be searching for Scout, but Emily and Dakota together had put the kibosh on that plan before they'd left. It wasn't fair how they'd both ganged up on her.

"There's no way we're letting you go out there. Especially alone!" Dakota blocked her way to the door outside, his blue eyes sparking with challenge.

"I can take care of myself. I have to find Scout."

"And we'll help you as soon as it's safe. But if you don't promise me right now that you'll stay put, I'll tie you to a

chair myself." Emily stood shoulder to shoulder with Dakota, hands on her hips.

Knowing Emily, she'd do it too. So what other choice had she had but to stay and distract herself by giving the place a thorough scrub down?

Allie jumped to grab her ringing phone, resting on the table in the middle of the room. Maybe someone had found Scout!

The picture of her mom and dad shone up from her screen. Again. Allie sucked in a deep breath. Better to get this over with.

"Hey, Mom."

"Allie, are you okay? Belle told us you were caught in a forest fire. Your father and I are worried si—"

"I'm fine, really. No need to worry." Of course, right then her throat seized and she had to cough.

"Maybe you should come home."

"No, really. I'm okay. Just a bit of a cough."

"We barely saw you at the wedding, and you didn't even come for Christmas. If you have the time off right now, we'd love to see you."

"I can't leave. My dog is—"

A long beep indicated another call. Belle.

For once, her best friend had perfect timing. "Sorry, Mom. I gotta go. I'm getting another call. But I promise I'll talk to you soon."

Her mother's sigh came through loud and clear. "All right, dear. Love you."

"Love you too. Bye." Allie quickly switched to Belle's call.

"Any word?" Belle asked.

"Nothing." Allie slumped into the nearest chair. "I posted on all the lost pet sites and groups in this area that I could. I called the local vets and animal shelter and left my number for them, but so far..." She couldn't finish the thought. The silence was eating her up inside.

"He'll show up. I asked the church prayer chain to pray for him. Plus, he's a smart dog."

He was. Too bad she wasn't a smart dog *handler*. Because she should've caught on way earlier that his obedience training wasn't the problem. Belle was right.

I haven't seen you once smile or look at him like you actually like him. Like you would with Dixie—

Maybe if she'd shown him a little more attention, he wouldn't have run off.

"So, what now?" Belle asked.

"Once the hotshot and smokejumper crews get back, I'll know more. All the roads around the burnt area were closed off, but hopefully by tomorrow I can go back and start looking for Scout. Until then, looks like I'm honorary basecamp mom. I've cleaned the kitchen top to bottom and have dinner in the oven."

Belle laughed. "I'm sure the microwave has never been cleaner."

"It was the first thing I attacked. It was so gross. All that food splatter—" Allie shuddered.

After a beat of silence, Belle spoke. "Are you sure you don't want me to come back and help you look for Scout? You don't have to do this alone."

Her best friend was starting to sound a lot like Dakota. "I'm not alone." Allie swallowed through the thickness in her throat. She wasn't any more alone than she deserved to be. "In fact, the house and base are so crowded, I'm not sure there'd be room if you did come."

"Sure you're not just saying that so I don't get in the way? Sounds like there's a few sparks with this cute firefighter who saved you. You should work on that."

Allie couldn't deny the thought had crossed her mind. But a flood of memories she couldn't escape, all the reasons she shouldn't, warred inside.

She must've stayed quiet too long.

Belle squealed. "Wait a second. Allie Monroe, are you falling for this guy?"

"Falling? We just met. Well, actually, we met last year. But I'm *only* staying for Scout."

A rumble sounded outside. "I gotta go, Belle. Sounds like the crew is here."

"I'll let you go, but only if you promise to tell me everything."

"Goodbyeee." Allie hung up on the sound of Belle's laughter. She swept an invisible crumb off the table and tried to ignore the flutter in her stomach. She was just worried about the meal turning out.

Emily's recipe wasn't complicated, but she'd never cooked for a crowd this big before. The nerves had nothing to do with seeing Dakota again.

Okay. Maybe they did. Not because of the *sparks* Belle teased her about. Because she hadn't given him an answer to his request to keep his past quiet—a desire she knew so well. So well, neither Belle nor her own big, perfect family had a clue why she'd left college and gotten into search and rescue.

She looked around, the ache of missing a furry friend to hold acute. It was too quiet without Dixie. Without Scout. The constant squeeze in her lungs tightened as she pictured his sweet, furry face.

Scout. Please be okay, boy. Please.

Because she couldn't go through losing another SAR dog.

She'd gotten *her* second chance through SAR. Obviously she was failing at the moment, but once she found Scout, she would be back in the game. How could she deny Dakota his own chance at redeeming himself?

The sound of trucks rumbling grew louder. Allie stepped outside just as the hotshot crew pulled up in a white van. A couple trucks with Jude County Hotshots emblems on the side followed.

Emily hopped out of the front seat and opened up the rolling garage door. "How's dinner coming along?"

"Haven't burned it yet."

"Good, cuz this is a hungry crew." Emily walked into the garage and plopped her helmet on a shelf. "Although, I should warn you about Dak—"

A young guy with dark hair and a goatee came up to them. "Who's th-this?"

"Allie, meet Mack," Emily said. "He and his big brother Hammer are from Trouble County. Mack here is the baby of the group."

Mack shot Emily a look of brotherly annoyance before he shook Allie's hand. "D-don't listen to h-her. No one else does." He smiled shyly before moving toward the building.

Allie watched the others hopping out of the van.

Emily nudged Allie's arm. "He'll be in the last truck, with Kane."

Heat infused Allie's cheeks. "I don't know what you're talking about."

"Brace yourself." Emily suddenly grew somber.

"It's not good. There was an accident on the break line."

The flutters erupted into a full-on panic. Something had happened to Dakota? She spied the shock of red hair coming from the other side of the van, but instead of walking on his own two feet, Dakota was being carried by three burly guys.

"Oh my gosh! Is he okay?" Without waiting for Emily's answer, Allie rushed up.

The guy she thought was Kane, the one that had been with Dakota and Emily earlier at the campground, had a grim look on his face. "Not sure if he'll make it."

"What?" Allie reached to help them. Dakota's face was covered in dirt and soot. He grimaced in pain as they jostled him. "What happened?"

"A tree fell on him." The man holding Dakota's right side had scarring on his cheek and his neck. His eyes were serious, concerned.

Allie gasped. "Shouldn't you be taking him to the hospital?"

Kane did a slow shake of the head. "We didn't think he'd make it that far. And he begged for the last thing he saw on earth to be your beautiful face."

Allie blinked.

"Knock it off, guys." Dakota swatted at the big blond with a beard. "Seriously, Ham. Put me down."

What was going on?

"Are you sure?" Ham asked. "We're only trying to help."

"Let. Me. Go," Dakota growled.

"All right, boys. You heard the man," Kane said.

All three men dropped him. Dakota hit the ground

and groaned. "Gee, thanks." He got up, albeit slowly, like he might truly be injured. But the others snickered and walked away. So it couldn't be too bad, right?

Dakota gave her a sheepish grin. "Don't listen to them. I'm fine."

"Are you sure?" She studied his face. That same handsome smile, eyes a startling clear blue. But they did pull a little. He was in pain.

He held his side as they moved toward the building. "I'm banged up a smidge, that's all. A dead tree fell. One of the branches got me. But I got right back up. No biggie."

"Oh." The tight coils around her middle loosened.

They passed one of the other firefighters—probably the oldest in the group, with his salt-and-pepper hair, but he couldn't be more than in his forties. Not for this job.

The man stuck his hand out. "You must be Allie. Emily said you were making supper for us. I'm Charlie Benning."

Allie shook his hand.

Dakota nudged her. "And the pretty boy coming up behind him is Orion. But don't let that baby face fool you; he's a hard worker."

Allie smiled at the younger guy behind Charlie as he walked past with a pack. Another couple dragged equipment from the trucks—a petite brunette woman with a serious scowl, and a tall guy with a full beard and dark coloring.

The woman's scowl softened as she approached Allie. "Heard about your dog. We're keeping an eye out for him."

"Thanks." Allie was about to offer a handshake, but the woman was already on her way inside.

Emily walked over and whispered, "That's the nicest I've *ever* seen Sanchez. I live with the woman, and she barely talks to me."

She definitely gave off a tough-chick vibe. "And who's the guy that went with her?" Allie asked Dakota, since Emily had started unloading her pack.

"That was Sax. Short for Saxon. He's pretty quiet. But all in all, it's been a good team so far."

"Masterson. Heads up!" someone yelled from behind her.

A water bottle came flying through the air. Dakota caught it one-handed. His arm lift revealed a long rip in the side of his shirt and blood on the white T-shirt underneath.

Allie gasped. "Dakota! That's not fine! You're hurt."

"It's a scratch. No big deal." He turned to the door. "The guys think I'm trying to get out of work, but I'm really trying to get them to pull their weight." His smirk revealed a long dimple in each cheek, reminding her of a young Robert Redford. Why did she have to have a thing for handsome gingers?

She gave herself a mental shake. *Keep it together, Monroe.* "Can I help you?"

He waved off her concern. "I'll be fine. Just need a bandage."

"Well, you're gonna have a hard time reaching it."

"I need to unload things here fir—"

Kane wandered past them, cutting him off. "Listen to the woman. We can handle the unloading without you." Kane hefted a couple of air tanks from the truck. "Seriously, go take care of yourself. You need to clean that cut so it doesn't get infected."

Dakota rolled his eyes. "Yes, Mom."

"At least someone is taking this seriously." Allie smiled at Kane, then settled her attention back on Dakota. "Let me check on something I have in the oven."

He nodded and left.

He was fine. She could breathe. A few minutes to gather herself while she checked on her mac and cheese and popped the cookies in the oven, then she'd be fine too. And maybe grab her own water bottle to help her parched throat.

A few minutes later, she found the infirmary room. She took a swig of water and opened the door. Dakota stood in the middle of the tiny room without his shirt on, a well-honed abdomen on full display with impressive shoulders and arms to boot as he tried to clean his wound. She choked on her water and started coughing.

"Whoa, you okay there?" Dakota's warm hand on her back did not help.

She coughed again and tried another sip of water. "I'm…dandy."

Dandy? Where had that come from? She sounded like her elderly neighbor Norman.

Her eye caught the gash on his side. "That is *not* a little scratch. You might need stitches."

Allie dragged over a chair and sat facing his shoulder. She held his arm away from his body, ignoring the warmth of his skin, and studied the angry, welted skin smeared with black ash. As long as she focused on his wound, not his massive presence that heated the room to tropical temperatures, she'd be great.

Deep purple bruising around the jagged cut said this was no scratch. As it was across the side of his ribcage, he would have difficulty cleaning it out alone. She donned gloves and grabbed the bottle of water he had on the counter next to a stack of paper towels.

"What are you doing?" He lowered his arm and shifted away on the chair, his cheeks pink.

"I'm helping."

"I don't need help, Allie. I'm—"

She nudged his arm back up. "Shush." She held the towels under the cut and proceeded to pour water on the wound.

"Ow!" He flinched, but after that he stayed still while she washed the grime away.

She tried to ignore the heat radiating from his body as she cleaned his side and the way the unique scent of smoke, hard work, and a distinctly male deodorant filled the room. With the most gentle touch she could, she wiped away the dried blood and dirt.

"It's not bleeding anymore." Allie avoided his eyes at all costs.

He cleared his throat. "Like I told you. No stitches necessary." He pulled away. "I can take it from here. I'm sure you've got better things—"

"Dakota."

He faced away from her and put his shirt back on. Apparently she wasn't the only one avoiding eye contact, because he was suddenly very interested in his boots. Or maybe it was the pattern on the floor.

The stubborn man needed treatment.

"It still needs some antibiotic ointment and a bandage. I'm no expert, but I could at least glue it closed." She held up the medicine, but he turned to face her, closing the space between them, and she caught the look on his face.

Time stopped.

"Allie." He cupped her cheek, so lightly she almost wondered if she was caught up in a dream. His touch set off a tingling sensation starting from her head and running down her spine. Her breath caught.

"I know I'm…wounded." His blue eyes softened. "But it's not your job to fix it."

"Maybe not. But I can help the healing process along."

He swallowed hard, his eyes reflecting some internal struggle going on inside him. Maybe it was his abusive father. Or his mother who'd lost herself in her own addictions. Either way, she got the sense Dakota wasn't used to someone taking care of him. He tried so hard to prove himself. The man who'd gone out of his way to keep her safe and rescue two little boys—that was the kind of man she should've waited for.

But she'd been so drunk with independence, so starved for someone to notice her, that she'd fallen for Christian instead. Christian, who'd convinced her to go against everything her family had instilled in her.

She'd given him so much. And she'd known better. She'd gotten exactly what she deserved. But Dakota had saved her life when he didn't have to. He'd walked beside her when he could've left her behind. He didn't deserve this kind of injury.

"Let me finish treating that cut, Dakota. I kind of owe you."

The corner of his lips quirked up in a half smile. "Owe me for what?"

"Did you forget already? You're my own personal hero today. You helped me find those boys. And survive a forest fire."

"Oh. That." His smirk brought back a playful vibe

but didn't completely dispel the electricity in the room. If anything, it made her like him even more.

"So maybe you let me help you this time, hmm?" She had a hard time keeping her thoughts straight as he looked at her that way, a smoldering desire mixed with vulnerability in his gaze. He finally nodded and pulled away so she could get back to treating him.

But goodness the man was pulsing with energy and appeal. She fought to concentrate on disinfecting and bandaging the cut while the magnetism of the last moments buzzed through her. She was holding the last strip of medical tape in her fingers when the smoke alarm went off.

The cookies!

As the whole crew, hotshots and smokejumpers, lounged outside behind the building, Dakota savored his last bite of cookie—even burnt, they were a hundred percent better than an MRE—and glanced at Allie across the picnic table. She laughed at something one of the girls said. Dusky sunlight caught the brunette strands, turning them auburn. Her eyes found him and she grinned.

Their moment in the infirmary blazed through his mind. Dakota standing in there, exposed, his bleeding wounds open for Allie to see. And rather than run away, she'd come close, bandaged him up, and called him a hero. It'd completely unarmed him. When was the last time someone had taken care of him like that?

He could fall fast for a woman like her. He should thank the good Lord above for the interruption.

The smoke alarm had been a nice touch. Very

appropriate for the way it'd almost felt like the room was on fire.

I tried, Lord, to take care of the injury myself, to not be drawn in by those gorgeous eyes of hers. So thank You for stopping me before I did something that I would regret.

He was too much like his father to be with someone as good as Allie Monroe. Sure, he'd had his share of girlfriends in the past—the strong, independent ones that didn't want a lot more than a good time. Temporary pleasures to distract himself.

Until God had got ahold of him, his body and soul battered and bruised, and shown him something more. Something eternal. He'd welcomed him with open arms, and it'd changed him forever. But he still had a lot of growing to do.

But maybe if he could get his act together, prove to her and not just the team that he was good, maybe somewhere down the line there could be chance for a future with someone like Allie. He could help solve this case and protect the boys to start.

She looked down at her phone and jumped up from the table. What was wrong?

He followed her to the side of the building, away from the chatter.

Allie spoke into the phone. "Hello? Jen?"

She looked at the screen, confused. "She didn't say anything. Just hung up."

"Maybe she dialed by accident."

"I thought I heard something in the background. A crashing sound."

"Try calling her back."

She did and got no answer. "I think we should go check on her."

"After what I heard about a murder in the forest, I

have questions of my own. Maybe if Ray isn't around, Jen will let us talk to Ethan again."

"What did you hear?"

"A body was found at another fire. A body someone tried to use the forest fire to cover up. And it had two gunshot wounds. One to the back. One to the head."

Her eyes widened. "You think Ethan was telling the truth? The scary man isn't Ray?"

"I don't know. But I think we should find out."

"I do too." The determined set to her mouth stirred something in him again. He always had liked a woman with guts. Someone who could stand up to the hard stuff and not cower like his mother had.

They took Allie's car to a run-down house on the edge of Ember. The white paint had long since turned a dull gray. Rust stained the siding beneath the spigot that poked out of the side of the house. The flower beds were overgrown, but the yard was mowed short and neat. A couple bikes lay in the grass. It was run-down but tidy.

Allie checked the address on her phone again. "This is the place." Her forehead wrinkled as she took a good look at the house and yard. Was she worried? Upset? Disgusted?

The house didn't look much different than the one he'd grown up in. And Allie probably had no clue what kind of darkness and filth was in a house like that. Not with all the stories she'd told him on their long ride about her good Christian family with all her brothers and sisters, their sing-alongs, backyard barbecues, and home-grown goodness.

She shouldn't be anywhere near someone like Ray

Haroldson. "When we get up there, you should stay behind me in case Ray gets upset."

"Or maybe *you* should wait here in the car. Because there is no *if*. When Ray sees you, he *will* get upset. And we don't want any more trouble for Jen or the boys. I'll go."

She might have a point, but—"There's no way I can sit here and let you face him alone." She didn't know what people like his father and Ray were capable of.

"Why don't you wait by the side of the porch. You'll be out of sight but close if anything happens."

He clenched his fist. "I don't like it. I should be the one—"

"We'll have the best chance at talking to Ethan if I go, and you know it."

Dang it. She was right. He calculated the distance to the steps. "Fine. But the second it gets iffy, you're out of there."

She waited until he was in place, his position in the grass obscured by a scraggly bush, before stepping up the porch steps and knocking on the door.

Ray's voice from inside was loud but muffled. Still, no one answered the door. Allie knocked again, louder this time. Dakota watched through the branches. The front door squeaked when Jen opened it and faced Allie. The woman's eyes widened slightly, and she quickly looked behind her.

"Who is it?" Ray yelled from somewhere in the depths of the house.

"It's nothing. I…I'll take care of it," Jen answered him in a shaky voice. She stepped onto the porch and almost closed the door behind her. She dropped her voice. "What are you doing here? You should leave."

"I got your call, Jen. Are you okay?" Allie kept her own voice low.

"I don't know what you're talking about."

"You called me."

"I didn't. It must've been the—"

"Jennifer! Who is it?"

Jen jumped and closed her eyes a second before yelling in the doorway. "I'm taking care of it!"

Movement sounded inside. Jen visibly tensed.

Allie reached for her hand. "Are you in trouble here? Where are the boys?"

Jen pulled away. "Like I said before, the boys are fine. They probably...called you. As a jo—"

The front door swung open and Ray appeared. His eyes were bloodshot. A blue-violet bruise was already showing around his eye where Dakota had socked him earlier.

"You! What are you doing here?" His voice roared. He shoved Jen aside.

Before Allie could say anything, Dakota came out of hiding. But he would keep his temper in check this time. "Calm down, Ray. We just want to talk to Jen and the boys. I have some questions about something they found in the forest."

Ray bristled as soon as he saw Dakota. "I told you to stay away from my family. Get out of here. Or else." His voice wasn't nearly as loud as before, but no one could miss the dark undertones of his threat.

But Dakota wasn't going to back down. "Someone called Allie. We want to make sure everyone is okay. And I'd like to talk to the boys."

"That's not gonna happen. And if you don't get—"

"Ray!" Jen tugged his beefy arm back toward the house. "It's fine."

"Is it?" He turned his mean glare on Jen. "And what is this about someone calling her?" He pointed to Allie.

"It must've been a prank."

Ray turned back to them. "There. No one called. And there's no way I'm letting you talk to the boys, so you best get. You're trespassing on my property."

Allie pulled Dakota back before he could react the way everything inside him was screaming to—with a flying right hook.

Again, Allie's strength took him by surprise. She managed to tug him down the porch steps to the crumbling sidewalk. "Kota, let's go. We don't want to cause any more trouble."

He was dying to show Ray what trouble he could cause, but she was right. Jen and the boys would probably pay for it. He held up hands in surrender and stepped back. "We're going."

They got back in the car and left.

"We've got to get them away from him." Allie squeezed the steering wheel, eyes fixed on the road, determination in every line of her face. "They can't stay there."

"You don't have to convince me." He watched the house grow smaller in the side mirror. "I know exactly what those boys are going through."

She glanced at him for a moment. "Is that what your father was like?"

He tried to shrug it off but couldn't. "Not exactly." In some ways, it'd been worse. "My dad was the sheriff in our county. People actually respected him. They didn't know any better. Because on the outside, everything looked fine. He was a stickler for keeping the yard neat, even though the porch was sagging and the house needed painting. There was never enough money for that kind of stuff, but he always made sure the grass was cut and the leaves were raked. That was my job. But it didn't matter how hard I tried, he would find fault with something. And he'd make sure I paid for it."

"I still can't believe your mom didn't do anything."

"She said I had to keep trying harder. That he was just trying to toughen me up."

Allie reached over and held his hand. Somehow, the touch loosened the need to hold it all inside.

"Once, I was about nine or ten years old, and I thought, 'Fine. Then I'll do it perfectly.' I went over the yard twice with the mower. I borrowed the neighbor's weed whip and everything. Spent the whole day pruning trees, trimming bushes, pulling weeds. There wasn't a blade of grass out of place or one stray twig on the lawn. Mom and I even scrounged up enough money to buy some flowers for the sad-looking flower bed we had by the porch. And I waited for him to get home. Waited to hear him say, finally, that he was proud of me, that I'd done a good job."

"What did he say?"

Dakota could still see his mom on the porch. She'd changed out of the muddy jeans into a nice dress and done her hair just for his father.

Look, Buck. Dakota spent his whole day tidying up the yard.

"He said, 'You cut the grass too short, boy. You just killed our lawn.' And he emptied his coffee mug on the flowers we'd just planted. Said they looked like—well, I'm sure you can guess."

"He didn't."

"That was Buck Masterson."

"Oh, Dakota." Her gentle voice reached deep inside, soothing the aches that'd never quite healed.

"It was my mom's flowers that got me. For once, she'd tried to help me get on Buck's good side. To see him desecrate them like that, I"—Dakota clenched a fist—"I got so mad I kicked the trash can. It tipped over and made a huge mess. And then Buck dragged me inside and let me have it." His mother had been next.

But Allie didn't need to know the particulars. The scars were mostly internal at this point.

"What did your mother do?"

Oh, that. "After Buck left, I went to check on her in her room." He could still remember the sour smell of sweat and alcohol. His mother curled up in a tight ball on the bed, wrapped up in her ratty bathrobe, her dress discarded in a heap on the floor. He'd approached quietly, hoping to find comfort together, come up with a plan to go, anything.

Mom, are you okay?

"She rolled over, looked me in the eye, and said...I was just like him. That if I hadn't lost it and kicked over the trash, he wouldn't have gotten so upset."

"Are you serious? She blamed you?"

Dakota looked out at peaks in the distance, clenching his molars tight. He loved the indignation in Allie's voice. But still, crazily enough, he didn't want to completely disparage his mother's name, like he needed to defend her. "She finally took me and left about a year later. But she was never the same."

"And she never told anyone?"

"Who would believe us? All the deputies worked under him. He had complete control over the paperwork and reports. And once we moved, there was no reason. She never talked about it again."

"I'm so sorry, Kota."

"It's in the past." He looked back at her. "But it was a great motivator when I went into law enforcement. I wanted to show everyone that I was *nothing* like my father. Not that I did a great job of it today."

Which was maybe why he was floundering so much after losing his job. It had been his whole identity. His way of undoing his past.

He might not be Benson PD anymore, but he could still help solve whatever was going on here in the wilderness around Ember and show his brother, Dani, and his nephews that he wasn't some washed-up addict. Maybe he didn't have to fight fires in the wilderness to do that. Maybe it meant working this case on the side, protecting two little boys in an all-too-familiar situation. Helping Allie find Scout.

"Dakota, you're one of the bravest, most honorable men I know. You asked me this morning for a chance to show me that you're one of the good guys. But I've always known that. And we all have things we're ashamed of. You have no idea of the things I've done."

She pulled over by the river that ran through the town.

"Oh, really? What horrible thing have you done?"

SEVEN

ALLIE WAS STILL FIXED ON DAKOTA'S STORY AS they walked along the river. Her heart broke for the little boy trying so hard to win the approval of his father only to be beaten. He might not have said it in so many words, but something told her he was still trying to protect her, not wanting to burden her too much with the darkness of his past.

Little did he know she had her own darkness. And unlike his childhood, she'd completely deserved it. But maybe he wouldn't feel so alone if he knew some of her own secrets.

"My family doesn't know this—I haven't even told my best friend Belle—but for a while, I moved in with my college boyfriend."

He stared at her, eyebrows lifted. "You?"

"Yeah. Me, the pastor's kid."

"You never told them?"

"How could I? It was the ultimate sin in my family. I was raised to know better. Do better." She looked out across the water at the foothills. "But I was convinced we were in love and that any day, he'd ask me to marry him. And the secrecy of it, it made me feel...special, like we had this tiny world all to ourselves. For a while it was good, because I was stupid enough to believe him when he said all we needed was each other, that he'd do anything for me."

"And here I thought with your big Christian family you were indestructible when it came to temptation." He said it with a wink, trying to lighten her load as always. There was no chastisement or condemnation. And in the quiet place between them, the past was clawing its way out, begging for release.

"Kota, you don't know the worst part." Her whispered voice cracked.

He took her hands and held them, gently rubbing his thumb over her knuckles. "You don't have to tell me anything, Allie. I'm no saint myself."

It was sweet of him, really. And she'd never be able to get the words out to tell him all of it, but maybe she could help him understand why she did the work she did. How desperately she needed to find her dog.

"Eventually the fantasy came crashing down on me, and it almost destroyed me."

"That bad, huh?"

"Let's just say my dog Dixie was the only good thing to come out of it."

"Dixie?"

"I adopted Dixie right before the breakup. After Christian left, I could hardly function. I'd made him, our relationship, everything. Without him, I didn't want to get up in the morning, but she gave me a reason. And when I didn't want to eat, I would do it because I didn't want anything to happen to her.

When I didn't want to leave the apartment, I would because I knew she needed exercise."

"Sounds like you took good care of her."

"I owe her my life. She gave me purpose again. And she was so smart. We were at a park where they were doing some SAR training. She jumped right in and passed their agility course on the first try. Watching them, I knew. That was what I was meant to do. I quit nursing school and started training with Dixie. She caught on so easily. And slowly, I began to build a new life."

"She's your hero."

Allie nodded.

"I'm so sorry you lost her," Dakota said.

"Me too. But hopefully, if I find Scout, we can finish our training and get back to work. He's a good dog too, but I didn't let myself get close to him. I didn't want to depend on him like I did Dixie. But I'm going to do better. I just need to find him."

"I promise, as soon as we can let you back there, we'll go and look for him. I truly believe he's still alive. But since we can't do anything today, what do you say we go find some more answers about this body Houston and Sophie found."

"How will we do that?"

"I want to talk to the medical examiner. My gut says something is going on here. And I wonder if Ethan and Nolan might be in the middle of it. If they really saw someone shot and killed, they could be in danger. If the ME has an ID, then we can see if Ethan recognizes the guy."

"What if that traumatizes him even more? Shouldn't the cops do that?"

"It would be a lot less invasive if you and I can talk to him first, confirm that it's true, and not send the sheriff on a wild-goose chase. I don't know how much he'll listen to us without proof."

It made sense. And since she couldn't do much more to look for Scout, at least they could be doing something to help the boys.

"Okay, so where do we go?"

They walked back to her SUV. Dakota directed her as she pulled back into the street. "What's the plan? You're just gonna walk into the medical examiner's office and start asking questions?"

"It's worth a shot. And I happen to know the ME."

Oh, well, if he knew the guy, maybe it wouldn't be so bad. Her phone rang again. This time her father. Probably trying to redouble the effort to guilt her into coming home.

"Do you need to get that?" Dakota asked her.

She silenced the call and stuffed the phone in her pocket. "It's just my dad. He'll leave a message."

"Are you sure?"

"Yup. We have more important things going on right now."

After a quick stop at a convenience store, she drove a few blocks to the heart of Ember and parked outside a brick building between the hospital and county courthouse.

At the reception area desk, Dakota asked to see Dr. Evans.

"It's kind of late, don't ya think?" Behind the counter, the stocky woman in a security uniform studied them.

"I know the doc isn't expecting us, but we met at a conference a few years ago out in Washington, where I'm from. I'm here for work though. Thought I'd stop by. And I happen to know Dr. Evans has a particular weakness for potato chips with cookie dough ice cream."

The woman smiled warmly as Dakota held up both items. "That's Dr. Evans all right. Okay, I'll take you back." She probably didn't get many visitors this time of day. And Allie could admit it—Dakota could be rather charming. Still, she shouldn't read much into his warm hand on her back as they followed the woman.

She led them down a hallway. "Why don't you wait in the office. I'll let the doctor know you're here."

They waited in a small room. One wall was a bookcase, the chairs were cheap plastic, and the carpet had seen better days but had recently been vacuumed, lines still running through it. Certificates with various colors of ink and fancy fonts hung on another wall. But it was the big picture window that captured her gaze. The gold sunlight of evening hit the mountains, turning them lavender, pink, and apricot. If not for the plumes of thick smoke rising from the forest, it would've been idyllic.

Lord, keep Scout safe out there. And I'd be just fine to never see another fire again.

The door opened and Dakota stopped pacing. Allie shouldn't judge someone based on their profession, but she had already conjured up a picture of this medical examiner. But instead of a middle-aged graying man with glasses and pasty white skin, a tall, gorgeous brunette wearing high heels walked in. Her darker skin and fabulous cheek bones hinted at Native American heritage.

This was the medical examiner? No wonder Dakota had wanted to "stop in."

Allie was still picking her jaw up off the ground when the woman walked up to Dakota and kissed him on the cheek. Her nails were glossy blue, her teeth bright white, and the lipstick could only be described as bombshell red. Well, wasn't that patriotic.

And here Allie sat in sweaty trail pants, a stained T-shirt, and clunky hiking boots.

"Dakota Masterson." Even the doctor's voice was sultry and sweet. "What are you doing in my neck of the woods? It's been a couple years since that conference in Seattle. I thought you'd forgotten all about me." She tossed a couple of the perfect beach waves over her shoulder, sending a whiff of strong perfume.

"Brought you a little something." Dakota held up the potato chips and pint of ice cream.

"Oh, you are an angel! I've got a late night ahead of me, and this will be just the thing to get me through." She took his offerings and put the ice cream in a tiny fridge hidden in one of the cabinets. "And who is this?" She smiled at Allie.

"Felicia, this is Allie Monroe."

Allie stuck out a hand and tried not to cringe when she noticed the dirt and ash still under her fingernails. But the beautiful doctor had perfect manners and didn't seem to notice as she shook hands.

"You'll have to excuse my appearance. I'm not usually dressed so fussy for work, but I had a court appearance earlier today and then meeting after meeting." She sat behind her desk. "I can't wait to get back into scrubs."

Movement from underneath the desk caught Allie's eye. The doctor quietly kicked off the high heels. Maybe she wasn't so bad.

"So, what can I do for you? Did you want a tour or—"

"I was hoping you could help us. We heard there was a body found a while back, shot and then burned. We ran across a couple of witnesses, so I was hoping to get a picture to confirm that they saw the same person."

"Are you on that case? All the way out in Benson?"

Dakota flashed her one of his handsome grins. "Just helping out while I'm here in town. Like I said, we have a couple kids who say they saw a guy get shot in the woods. And then I heard about the body found out near that ranch."

Wait a minute. The woman was assuming he was still a cop. And although he hadn't outright lied, he was withholding the truth.

"Let me check..."

Allie tried to get Dakota's attention while the doctor started typing on her keyboard.

He was too busy looking at *Felicia*.

"Psst." Allie shot him low whisper.

He gave her a slight shake of the head and returned to smiling at the doctor. "So, did you ever finish remodeling your kitchen?"

She laughed. "You remember talking about that?"

"I remember being impressed that a woman knew

the difference between an impact driver and a cordless drill."

While the two of them chuckled together, Allie had the insane urge to kick something. All because some cute guy had shown her a little attention and now was focused on someone else. What was happening to her?

A printer behind the doctor started whirring and soon spat out two pages. Felicia handed them over to Dakota. "Here you go. It took a while, but we did ID him finally. Army Ranger Kurt Paulson. There was no next of kin to notify."

"An Army Ranger?" After studying the picture, Dakota passed it to Allie.

The photo was of a rough-looking man with dark features, a military haircut, and dress uniform. The boys had mentioned him wearing a necklace of some kind.

A sudden chill ran down her back, and she looked up from the paper. "Was he really shot *and* burned? Is that odd?"

Dr. Felicia held up two fingers. "He was shot twice. Once in the back and once in the head, then he was burned and left in an area where the fire was approaching. We're pretty sure the body was moved there, that it wasn't the initial crime scene. The sheriff believes he was executed and someone tried to cover it up."

So Ethan and Nolan very well could've been the last ones to see this man alive. And if someone had gone to all the trouble of killing an Army Ranger, they probably wouldn't have any qualms about silencing two little boys.

Allie locked eyes with Dakota. "We have to find the boys."

Dakota was completely on board with Allie. They left the building with the pictures. Now to find Ethan and Nolan and keep them safe.

"We need to go to the cops, right?" Allie asked.

What? Hadn't they already been through this? "First we talk to Ethan and Nolan."

"I know that's what we planned, but—"

"Allie, we have the picture. We need to see if this is the man they saw. This is no made- up story about Ray. Those boys actually witnessed a murder. And the killer is still out there somewhere. We have to figure this out."

She stopped on the sidewalk and folded her arms across her chest. "But you don't have the authority to do stuff like that. You're not a cop anymore. And you lied to Felicia. You're not officially on this case."

"What are you saying?"

"That it's not your job anymore. And I want to protect Ethan and Nolan just as much as you do, but I bet that doctor would've still given you the information if you'd been up front with her. And"—she let out a short breath and looked him straight in the eye—"at some point you've got to come to terms with the fact that that part of your life is over."

He tried hard not to wince at that. Over. Finished. Washed up. Yeah, that all fit him to a T. But it didn't mean he had to like it. Besides, how exactly did one come to terms with losing one's whole identity?

Allie stepped closer and laid her small hand on his

arm. "You don't have to be a SWAT guy to help others. The world still needs you, Dakota. It just might look a little different now. That's not a bad thing."

Wasn't it? Why did it seem like no matter what he did, it wasn't enough? But somehow, the way Allie looked up at him, her hazel eyes filled with something he'd been desperately longing for, he began to hope. Maybe there was some other way to prove to Will and the world that he wasn't just a hotheaded addict who'd thrown his life away. Maybe he did have something to offer an amazing woman like Allie.

And he hated disappointing her. "I'm sorry I didn't admit to Felicia that I wasn't with the PD anymore. It's…not something easy to say. I ruined a great career."

"Dakota, you fought back against an addiction. That takes incredible strength. You don't need to hide it. You should be proud of who you are and what you've accomplished. *I'm* proud of you."

She was proud? Of him? After everything she'd witnessed?

The question must've shown in his face, because Allie reached up, her small hand brushing his jaw, her eyes alight. "There's a lot more to you than a badge or your résumé. You're a good man, Dakota."

Her words stoked something deep inside, feeding a hunger he'd tried so hard to ignore. How did she do that? They barely knew each other.

But he wanted to know her. He wanted to help her, show her that not every guy was like her ex. He wanted something true, someone to build a life with, a family. Maybe God had brought him all the way out to Montana just to reconnect with her.

His gaze fell to her lips. Everything inside screamed to kiss her.

Maybe someday, but not yet. He still had a ways to go to be the kind of man she deserved, not to mention he had a job to do and a couple of boys to protect.

Dakota cleared his throat. "Thanks. What do you say when things calm down a bit we go out and get dinner? Maybe not barbecue though."

Allie laughed. "I'd like that." She grew somber, her grin fading. "But what do we do now?"

Right. Back to the task at hand. He relaxed his clenched jaw. "I need to talk to the boys. I want to see if they recognize this Paulson guy."

"Yeah, but Ray—"

"If I know guys like Ray, he'll be drinking by now. If we're lucky, he's doing it somewhere else other than home. So why don't we drive by the house. If we see his truck, we'll think of something else. But if it's not there, we'll see if Jen will let us ask Ethan some questions."

"Okay," she said with a quick nod. "Let's go."

Her confidence rubbed off. It was nice to have her believe in him at least this much. Maybe she was right and he had some things to figure out with his career, but for now, he had a case he very much wanted to close, official or not.

The sun was setting as they turned onto the Haroldsons' street.

Allie pointed at the house in the distance. "Is that smoke?" A tree on the corner of the lot blocked their view of the back of the home, but the columns of gray-black smoke marring the sherbet-colored sky couldn't be missed.

"Hurry."

They pulled up to see flames consuming the corner of the roof. Ray's truck was nowhere to be seen. As soon as Allie parked, Dakota sprinted to the front door and pounded. "Anyone home?" He jiggled the knob. Locked. "Ethan! Jen!"

The boys came from the side of the house. Ethan limped still. "We're here!"

Allie rushed over to them. "Where's your mom? What happened?"

Tears coursed down Nolan's face. Ethan kept a strong arm around his brother's shoulders. "We just came back from a bike ride and Ray was gone. We saw the fire, but we can't find Mom! And the door is locked."

"Call 911," Dakota told Allie. She ran for the car and came back with her phone. "I'm going to find a way inside, but I need you to keep these guys safe. Maybe they should wait in the car—"

Ethan pulled away from them. "We need to find my mom!"

"We can't do that if you and Nolan aren't safe," Dakota tried to explain.

Allie said, "Can you stay here on the sidewalk?"

"Please, just find her." Ethan hiccupped, sending a shudder through his whole body.

Fine. He didn't have time to argue. "Allie, make the call. I'm going in." Dakota rushed back to the porch. The fire seemed to be in the back of the house somewhere. After a quick touch to make sure the handle wasn't hot, Dakota sent a swift kick to break the locking mechanism. The front door swung open and smoke poured out.

"Jen! Jen Haroldson?" Dakota pulled his shirt up over his nose and walked in.

He stayed low to the ground and searched the living area. Nothing. The steps leading upstairs were already on fire. The kitchen was engulfed in flames.

Dakota got as close as he could and didn't see anyone. Heat seared his skin and pushed him back.

Jen was nowhere to be found, and if he stayed in here much longer, he could die.

EIGHT

THE ONLY THING SHE COULD DO WAS WAIT.

Allie knelt on the sidewalk with an arm around each boy, their small frames the only solid thing she could hold on to. Smoke poured out the front door and drifted up. Sirens screamed in the night. The whole roof was on fire now. And Dakota was still in there. She'd already called the dispatcher and hung up with them. The longer they waited, the harder Nolan started crying.

Allie needed to distract them.

No, what Allie needed was for Dakota to walk out that front door in one piece with Jen Haroldson. But since that wasn't happening…

"Mommy!" Nolan screamed and shot off into the shadows. Allie lunged after him and fell to the sidewalk as he disappeared around the corner of the house.

Ethan ran after him.

"Boys!" Allie jumped to her feet and took off.

If they kept clear of the burning structure, they'd be okay.

Giving the burning house a wide berth, she skirted

around the corner to the side yard. "Ethan! Nolan! Come wait with me out front. It's not safe back here."

Between the roaring fire and nearing sirens, she could barely make it out, but she could still faintly hear one of the boys shouting from the backyard. She turned the corner...

Fire ate up the whole rear of the house. Flames shot out the windows. Sparks flew. Walls and siding were consumed by yellow-and-orange tongues. For a moment Allie couldn't move. Couldn't turn away from the destruction. How had this happened?

Dakota was in there somewhere.

But Nolan's cry pulled her back to the moment. The yard was lined with a privacy fence. A tree in the corner kept that part of the yard in the shadows. She found Ethan on his hands and knees.

"Ethan! Where's Nolan?"

Ethan pointed under the tree.

Fire trucks pulled onto the street, the sirens deafening now. Allie lifted the branch and gasped.

There, huddled against the trunk of the tree, was Jen Haroldson. Her eyes opened as they came closer but didn't focus. Blood caked the side of her face from a gash on her temple. Nolan cried in her lap.

Allie moved closer. "Nolan, I need to be super gentle. Your mom is hurt, and we need to get her help. Ethan, go call one of those firefighters in the front. Tell them Dakota is inside and your mom is back here and needs medical attention."

The boy nodded and ran off. Nolan cuddled up in Jen's lap.

"Jen, can you hear me?" Allie hunched over to avoid the low tree branches.

Jen moaned in response. At least this time she kept her eyes open and made eye contact. Her thin arms wrapped around Nolan.

"Hey, we're getting you some help, okay?"

A couple EMS workers ran over with Ethan. Allie coaxed Nolan into her own arms and backed out of the way. After a quick assessment, they shifted Jen out from under the tree and lifted her onto the stretcher.

Thank goodness Nolan gave her something to hold. She held him close and stood by Ethan. Surely Dakota was out of the house by now. He needed to know they'd found her.

They followed the EMS personnel back to the front yard. Two more paramedics took the boys to one of the rigs to look them over. While they headed to the ambulance with Jen, Allie stopped in the corner of the yard. Firefighters raced around, some dragging a hose across the grass, others talking into radios. Police pushed back onlookers. But nowhere did she see Dakota. She ran to the first firefighter she could find.

"Excuse me. Have you seen—"

"Sorry, ma'am. I have to ask you to leave." He gently pushed her back and turned back to talking to his coworker, an older man with a beard.

"No, wait. Someone is in there!"

They both looked at her. The one with a beard asked, "Who?"

"My friend, Dakota. He's a hotshot. He went in to check on Jen Haroldson. This is her place." Hadn't Ethan told them?

The firefighter shook his head. "Ma'am, are you

sure? Someone already checked and said there's no one inside right now."

"He went in there! I saw him. You have to get him out!"

At that moment, fire shot out the front window, and glass shattered on the porch. Everyone ducked.

The other firefighter pulled Allie farther from the house. "You need to stay back. We're getting water on it now. As soon as we can get inside safely, we'll—"

"No! That's not acceptable!"

A warm hand on her arm held her back. "Allie."

She spun around. Dakota stood there, ash smeared across one cheek. His eyes were red and his hair was mess, but she'd never seen him look better. "Oh my goodness!" She grabbed him in a tight hug. "You're okay. I thought..."

She squeezed her eyes tight against the sting of tears. He smelled of smoke and soot, but she didn't care. He was alive. She almost collapsed with relief.

"It's okay. I'm here." He whispered the words in her ear.

She blew out a shaky breath and forced her muscles to relax. Once she was certain she could stand on her own, she stepped back. "I'm sorry. I was...worried about you. But you're okay?"

He smiled and she soaked it in. "Yeah. I'm okay." He pulled her back against his chest.

For a moment he just held her close. His embrace helped melt away the icy tentacles of fear that had wrapped around her. He was solid and strong, and Allie couldn't deny the appeal. His arms felt like home.

"How did you get out?" Allie asked.

"I didn't stay long. I saw a blood trail leading out

the side door and figured Jen got out." Someone bumped into them. Dakota pulled back a little. "And it looks like you found her." He pointed to the ambulance, where they were lifting Jen inside.

"The boys did. I'm not even sure how. But we should find them. Nolan's been inconsolable."

"Let's take them to the hospital so they can see their mom. I'm sure we'll have to wait while she's checked out. Then we can ask them if Paulson is the same guy they saw in the forest. But first, I need to talk to the fire chief."

"Why?"

"Someone set the fire on purpose."

"How do you know?"

"There was an empty can of paint thinner on the kitchen floor."

Allie gasped. Who would've set that fire? And Jen's injury. What had happened to her?

Dakota left to find the chief. She longed for her dog, a steady and calm presence to reassure her. But at least Dakota was here and okay.

But Ray was somewhere out there too.

Maybe now Jen would listen and tell her what was going on in their home.

Dakota could still smell the clean citrusy scent of Allie's shampoo from when she'd hugged him. Her arms had squeezed him tight. And when she'd pulled back, her eyes had been shimmering, like she'd been truly worried about him and a little teary.

Not that he should read anything romantic into it.

Even though she'd agreed to go out with him sometime.

Still, he couldn't deny how the heart in his chest swelled at the sight of her. Especially right now, as she held Ethan's hand and they walked into the hospital emergency department for the second time today. Nolan rested in Dakota's arms, his little body still shuddering every so often. Dakota tried not to cough all over the kid, but he'd inhaled too much smoke today. His side hurt like crazy too. But Nolan was tired and worried, and Allie shouldn't have to carry him.

After settling the boys with Allie in the waiting area, Dakota went in search of sustenance. There had to be a vending machine somewhere. Once the boys had had something to eat and were calmer, he could ask them about Paulson. He wandered into a small alcove off to the side of the hospital gift shop, the fluorescent lights of the pop machine glaring.

Ethan and Nolan were good kids. So why did Jen stick around a guy like Ray? Because maybe if he could figure that out, he could understand his own mother's choice to stay with Buck for so long. Maybe she'd thought she could change him at first. But after the first few times of striking her, wouldn't it have been obvious? Some men didn't change. He probably should be glad she'd left him eventually, but ten years under a man like that did a lot of damage. Had anyone reached out to his mom like Allie was doing for Jen? Offered her help or a way out? Would she have turned them down?

No matter how much he tried, for the life of him he couldn't understand how a mother could allow her own child to be harmed.

Thank goodness for strong women like Allie.

I don't know what You have in store for her, Lord, but I'd like to be worthy of a woman like that. I know I'm not there yet. But with Your help, I could be. I could be Your guy.

He punched the buttons and grabbed the sports drinks that dropped down. After finding some chips and protein bars, he brought them back to the others.

"Any word on Jen?" he asked quietly by Allie's ear.

"Nothing yet."

But soon after chowing down on the snacks, the doctor came by to give a report that Jen was going to be okay. She wanted to see the boys, but they needed to clean her up and run another scan first.

Happy for the chance to see his mom soon, Nolan crawled into Allie's lap with a picture book from one of the tables and asked her to read it. Ethan's thin shoulders finally rested against the back of his chair as the doctor left.

"Your mom's gonna be okay. We'll stay with you until we know you're safe. Okay?" For some reason Dakota wanted to reiterate that.

Ethan nodded. He was a strong kid. Probably because he had to be. And now that he didn't have to worry about his mother, this might be a good time to get some answers. The cops would be here any moment. He could protect the boys best if he knew what they were dealing with.

Dakota pulled out the paper with Kurt Paulson's picture and caught Allie's eye before she started reading. She gave him a slight nod yes.

"Hey, Ethan, can I show you something? I was wondering if you could help me out."

"Help how?"

He showed Ethan the picture. "When you talked about the scary man you said you saw in the forest, was he with this man?"

The boy's eyes grew wide. "Yeah! That's the one the scary man shot!"

The older woman sitting next to her husband by the wall perked up at Ethan's loud voice.

Great. Busybodies. Dakota lowered his voice. "Are you sure?"

Ethan nodded emphatically. "The tall ponytail guy—he has a tattoo of a gun and flag going up his arm—he was yelling at that man in the picture. When he walked away, he shot him in the back. This guy fell, and then the man shot him again."

Dakota's gut clenched. So it had been the murder they'd witnessed. The woman listening leaned in, probably hearing every single word. Allie paused in her reading and shared a look of concern. She turned the page and kept Nolan occupied.

Dakota looked back at the older boy. "What happened then?"

"We ran away. We…we tried to tell my mom, but she already had stuff going on. And I wasn't technically supposed to be off the trail." Ethan's brows dipped in worry. "Are we in trouble?"

Not if Dakota had anything to say about it. This kid was a victim, not a troublemaker. "No, you're not in trouble, bud. But we're going to have to talk to the sheriff so he knows. They're trying to find the man who shot him." He nodded toward the photo. "You could be a big help in solving this case. But we also want to make sure you and your brother stay safe. Did the tattooed guy see you?"

"I don't know. He yelled like he saw us, but we were pretty far away and uphill. And we ran fast."

"What are you doing with those boys?" Ray's yell cut across the room.

Dakota glanced across the waiting area and saw the boys' stepfather at the entrance of the hospital. He stumbled in on his unlaced work boots, drips of something on his dirty T-shirt, and ran right into a chair. He swung a heavy arm and shoved the chair out of his way. The older couple sitting on the other side of the room watched, mouths agape.

Dakota jumped to his feet to put himself between Ray and the boys, but he didn't move forward. He needed to be the clear-headed one here and defuse the situation.

"Ray, calm down. We're just keeping an eye on them while Jen is being treated."

"We don't need any help from you." The bald man lumbered forward. Even with twenty feet between them, Dakota could smell the cigarette smoke and alcohol. Great. He was a belligerent drunk.

The older woman in the loud purple-and-green shirt stood and approached Ray. "Now, Raymond, you're in no shape to—"

"Shut up, Betty. No one asked you. You're a mean old gossip, and no one cares what you say."

The man in a matching green golf shirt came up to the woman and stood beside her. "That's no way to talk to my wife. You get out of—"

Ray pushed the man aside. "You better stay out of my way, old man." He kicked another chair away.

Nolan whimpered somewhere behind Dakota, and Allie tried to soothe him. Ray was terrifying the boys. Hopefully Allie had grabbed Ethan too. Dakota couldn't risk looking or letting his focus drop. He was about to move in when the sheriff walked in with the same deputy that had been here earlier.

"Ray Haroldson, stand down," the sheriff said.

"This ain't none of your business," Ray slurred.

"Sheriff, I insist you arrest this man!" The older woman stood and pointed at Ray. "He's covering for a murderer and silencing these children."

If that lady didn't shush and stay out of this, things were going to escalate. Ray was on the verge of exploding. The vein on the side of his head pulsed fast. Dakota was poised to whisk the boys away if the man came any closer.

"Betty, Robert, I'll take your statements in a second," the deputy said.

Betty huffed. "Well, I never—"

Her husband grabbed her hand. "Woman, would you sit down. Can't you see he's got this?"

The sheriff walked up to the drunk. "Let's go, Ray. You need to sleep this off."

"No one is taking those boys away from me! Where's Jennifer?" His loud voice boomed. He tried to step closer to Ethan and Dakota, but the sheriff reached for his arm to stop him. The deputy closed in on the other side of Ray.

"I suggest you leave the boys alone right now. You're drunk and you drove here. According to Tracy, you made quite the ruckus at the bar tonight."

Ray swung at the sheriff and missed. He collapsed to the floor, where he blinked up at them.

"That was the wrong move, Ray." The sheriff looked to his deputy. "He can sleep it off in holding."

"Sure thing, boss." The deputy cuffed Ray and hauled him away.

The older couple closed in.

"It's such a shame." The older woman tsked. "What kind of trouble did he cause at the bar?"

Sheriff Hutchinson held up a hand. "Let me stop you right there, Betty. Robert, do you want to press charges?"

The older man shook his head.

"Then I'm done here."

Betty huffed. "I just want help, Sheriff. I know everyone around these parts." She turned to Dakota and Allie. "So, what happened with Jen Haroldson? Did that man hurt her? Is that why you're here with the boys?"

"I'm sorry. We've got to find a bathroom to wash this guy off." Allie picked up Nolan. "Ethan, why don't you come with me." They went to the restroom on the other side of the waiting area.

Robert tugged his wife back to the corner they'd been in earlier, but their obvious interest in the conversation had Dakota gesturing to the sheriff to move as far away from them as he could.

"Sheriff, I think you should talk to Ethan when he gets back. He witnessed a murder in the forest not too far from the campground."

"A murder?" The sheriff thankfully kept his voice low too. "What makes you say that?"

"He said he saw a man shot and killed. And I heard a dead body was found recently. It matches Ethan's story—"

"Let me stop you right there. I'm familiar with Ethan's stories. He's called the office multiple times with reports of bad guys. I think we know who the real bad guy is he's worried about."

"This isn't a story about Ray. I'm talking about that Army Ranger."

"And how do you know about that?" The sheriff's eyes narrowed.

"I heard…something." He didn't want Felicia to get in trouble for sharing information. "Something is going on out there in the forest."

The sheriff folded his arms across his chest and faced Dakota. "I appreciate you keeping an eye on Jen's boys, but that's where your involvement ends. If it will make you feel better, I'll talk to the boy tomorrow. It's late and he's been through enough. Now, if you don't mind, I've got a drunk and disorderly to book. But stay out of my murder case."

The sheriff left with a nod to the lady in scrubs behind the counter.

So much for working with the local law enforcement to get some answers. What was it going to take for someone to take Dakota seriously?

Because once a cop, always a cop…at least, as far as he was concerned. He'd quit voluntarily because that was better than being fired. But he wasn't walking away.

Not this time.

NINE

DAWN WAS A WELCOME SIGHT. ALLIE DIDN'T THINK she could take any more hours lying awake in the dark. She quickly dressed and quietly made her way to the kitchen. Time to go find Scout.

It being their first free day in over two weeks, the other girls in the house slept in. While Allie waited for the coffee to brew, she looked out the small window over the sink. She could only see a faint outline of the mountains thanks to the smoke and haze still hanging in the atmosphere. Even this far from the fire. And poor Scout. He was out there.

But Dakota had promised to help her look for him today. Dakota, who was quickly taking over a lot of space in her head. That little moment on the front porch when he dropped her off last night replayed over and over again.

He'd put the car in Park, and she'd watched the muscles in his forearm flex. They'd walked to the door and stood there, an electric current in the silence around them.

He'd chuckled quietly, and she'd watched the

humor in his eyes as he leaned toward her. Was he going to kiss her?

He'd lifted a hand and brushed her hair. "You have a bit of a leaf here. Must be from finding Jen." Emily and Jojo had busted out laughing at something inside.

Hello, reality crash.

He had her forgetting things she shouldn't forget. And if he really knew everything? It would only mean heartbreak in the end. She'd better get her head on straight before she spent the whole day with him. He was handsome and heroic, but she couldn't afford to lose her heart to him.

She went out to the front porch and sat on the bench swing with her coffee and her Bible. The sun rose in the sky, a weird neon-red sphere as it peaked over the mountains in the east. After Allie had commented on the same eerie color at sunset last night, Emily had said it was only because of the smoke in the air. But the old rhyme Grandma Kay used to say came to mind.

Red at night, sailor's delight. Red in the morning, sailor take warning.

At least in the daylight Allie could think straight. Between the fire and Ray's drunken outburst, she couldn't settle her nerves. Add to the mix the confusion of being around Dakota Masterson, and it was good as slamming down a six-pack of energy drinks.

He was danger to her heart for sure. Her heart rate raced every time she remembered the almost-kiss.

She was foolish enough to imagine what it would've been like if the sudden laughter hadn't broken the spell. And now she couldn't separate fantasy from reality.

Allie groaned and dropped her head back against the porch swing. Three yellow finches crowded at a bird feeder hanging from the eaves.

At least Ethan and Nolan were safe…for the moment. Jen's sister had come for the boys soon after the sheriff left, since Jen needed to stay in the hospital. But like Dakota, Allie couldn't shake a sense of foreboding over what might happen next. Those boys had witnessed a murder. And no one seemed to care except herself and Dakota.

But what could they do about it?

She needed Scout. Almost twenty-four hours since she'd seen him, and still no sign of her dog. She sent Dakota a text. If he wasn't up yet, he would see it when—

Her phone rang.

She stared at his name for a second, biting her lip. *Answer it.* She was the one who'd contacted him first. "Hey, uh…morning."

"Of course I'm up." His slightly raspy morning voice sent warm swirls through her middle.

Oh boy. Probably, spending more time with him would only get her into trouble. And yet, he was the only one who was crazy enough to go with her. He'd proven that. But when they'd had a moment alone…

He hadn't kissed her.

She could keep this about business if he didn't need the personal part. "I know it's your day off, but I was wondering if the roads were open and we could look for Scout. And since we lost him by that cabin, maybe we can start there and find evidence to corroborate Ethan's story."

"I like the way you think, Monroe. I'm in."

"Great. I'll come pick you up."

Within an hour they were in the campground parking lot again, although this time it was completely vacant. The air still smelled like smoke. The main area with all the campsites remained unburnt thanks to the quick work of the hotshot crew, but just beyond the office building, where the trails started, was a different story. No green trees or underbrush.

Allie stepped over a thick trunk that had fallen across the trail. "It looks so different." Scorched skeletons of pine and spruce stood. Everything was covered in gray ash. It was like walking in a black-and-white photo.

Using a hiking stick as they walked, Dakota checked for embers and hot spots.

They'd have to start by the caves where they'd found the boys if they wanted to find the route to that cabin. Remembering how protective Ethan was reminded her of Dakota's big brother Will. She didn't know a lot about their past, but maybe learning about it would help her to understand Dakota more.

"You said your mom didn't tell you about Will until she died, but you seem so close now. How did you find him?"

"I didn't at first. When my mom told me that Will didn't want anything to do with us, I believed her. He had a different mother, and there's a big age gap. I wasn't born until he had moved out. It made sense when she said he thought he was better than us."

"That doesn't sound like Will at all."

"Yeah, but back then I didn't know that." He shrugged a shoulder. "I know better now."

"So what happened?"

"I saw his wedding announcement in the local paper. Being a hotheaded teenager, I thought I'd show up and cause a scene." He winced. "Come to find out, Will never knew about me either."

Allie watched a bird flit across the trail. "Wow."

"Yeah, my father never told him I existed or that he had been with my mom. After that, Will invited me to spend summers with him and Dani. I think he tried to make up for our dad, you know?"

"Now *that* sounds like the Will Masterson I know."

"He was always the one Masterson man that had it all together."

"Did you look up to him?"

Dakota nodded. "What's not to admire? He was with Homeland Security for years; now he and his wife do search and rescue, which you know. He's an upstanding guy. Family man. Not having the greatest example as a father, I guess I looked up to Will quite a bit, and I love his twins. My nephews are the best." His voice grew quiet. He snapped off a dead branch and studied it. "I'm surprised you willingly drove me anywhere after you saw me lose it with him."

"It was Will who told me I could trust you."

Dakota's head jerked up.

"He told me you were a good guy struggling with an addiction and taking it out on him."

"He knew I was doing that?"

"Have you ever talked about it with him?"

Dakota looked down again, using the stick to sift through the ashes. "I haven't brought it up. I owe him so much. He paid for that rehab, arranged the ride. I've been to see him a few times since, but…I need to do more. I want to use my salary as a hotshot and my sign-on bonus to pay him back. And I need to get my life together, show him that everything he did wasn't wasted. I owe him that at least."

"He's your brother, Dakota. You don't have to prove anything."

"I need to make things right though. I've got some money saved up. I'm getting there."

"I understand wanting to pay him back, but don't you think a relationship is more than that? He loves you unconditionally. Dani and the kids too. Samuel and Joshua are always talking about Uncle Kota. I think they look up to you. Why else do you think they signed up for the teen fire-training camp…what's it called?"

"Wildlands Academy." He jabbed his stick on the ground, not making eye contact.

"Dani dropped them off last month, and I don't think it's too far from here. You should go visit them."

He looked at her and stilled. "I'll think about it."

They turned away from the trail and hiked down the slope, the same way they had yesterday. Thank goodness for the little bit of rain that had fallen last night. With the fire to the west of town and the wind pushing the smoke away, the air was cleaner.

"What about you? Think you'll ever tell your family about Christian?"

"And taint the Monroe name in Twin Valley, Idaho? That would be a bad idea."

Dakota flipped over another log. It smoked, a thin line of orange outlining the embers under it. He led her around the area, quiet for a minute. They stood on a small ridge, looking out over the burnt trees and blackened boulders.

"Is that why you don't answer your dad's calls? Or go visit them?"

Allie lifted a shoulder and avoided his direct gaze. "I dunno. Maybe."

He stayed silent for a moment. Poked at the ground with his stick. "When I finally got the guts to admit to Will I'd been kicked off the SWAT team, it was humiliating, but it was also the first step toward healing. Of course, I didn't handle it well when he insisted I needed rehab. Obviously. I wasn't expecting an ankle injury to lead to a painkiller addiction, and I did my best to hide it. No one was fooled. I know how things just sneak up and take over our lives without us realizing it. But the way you talked about your family on that car ride, it sounded like you missed them. Like you have a good thing there. I think you're hurting yourself not telling them."

No way. "You don't get it. My family is... complicated."

"Aren't they all?"

"Yeah, but my father is the pastor at a church. I would ruin his reputation. And like you said, God's forgiven us, so why dredge all that up again when I've put it all behind me?"

"I'm the last person who should be giving anyone advice. I just know how heavy it is to carry that kind of thing around. And it's not like you have to shout it from the rooftops. But it sounded like you used to be close with your family. Wouldn't the people who love you the most understand?"

Would they? Not if they knew everything. Dakota didn't even know everything. No one did.

But his touch and his words reached the tender places of her heart, infusing some light in those dark places. He tugged her hand to stop and faced her. The fire might've gone out in the forest, but the air between them heated like an inferno.

Dakota brushed a strand of hair off her forehead and tucked it behind her ear, setting off shivers across her skin. He traced her brows, her cheek, and moved to her jaw.

"Thank you for coming out here with me and for helping me keep the boys safe," she said softly.

Somehow, the space between them shrank. Allie didn't know if she moved or Dakota did. But he was still too far away.

He leaned forward, his nose gently nudging hers. They stayed there a few seconds, sharing the space, until she couldn't take it anymore.

She tilted her face up, her lips finally meeting his. Tentative at first, then hungry for more, she fisted her hands in his shirt and pulled him closer.

He got the hint.

His arms wrapped around her, molding her to his body, and he met her kiss for kiss. The moment tasted of coffee and cinnamon and smoke. *Please don't let it end.*

Colors and light flashed across her mind as she soaked in Dakota's passion and energy. The man was strength and masculinity and heat. So much heat. And she couldn't get enough.

A dog barked in the distance, and reality crashed in. Again.

Dakota pulled away, though not completely. He still held her.

Allie didn't want to open her eyes. She wanted to stay there in that perfect moment, try to recapture the warmth they'd shared, but the spell was broken. She looked around.

"Did you hear that?" Dakota asked.

The bark was closer now. Wait! She knew this bark.

She pulled out of Dakota's arms. "It's Scout!"

Dakota missed Allie as soon as she left his arms. But the joy in her face when she realized it was Scout barking was unmistakable.

Please, let it be Scout.

Allie ran over to the edge of the ridge and stopped. She cupped her hands to her mouth and yelled. "Scout!"

Her voice echoed back, nothing else but silence.

"That had to be him, don't you think?"

Before he could answer, something on the ground caught his eye. "What's that?"

She kicked aside the ashes and revealed a dark-blue cloth. "It's a bandana."

Dakota used his stick to lift it up. "That might be blood on it." He pulled a plastic baggie out of his backpack and picked it up with the bag covering his hand.

Allie opened the GPS app on her phone. "We're not that far from where we were with the boys."

"I think we're close to the cabin we saw when we were running from the fire."

They used the GPS to navigate to a clearing. Everywhere they turned, it all looked the same. Burnt devastation. Husks of trees. Smoldering piles of ash.

Every now and then they called for Scout, but there was no more barking.

Allie's lips pinched tight after calling again without an answer. Maybe Dakota could keep her from getting discouraged.

"Did you have dogs like Dixie or Scout growing up?"

"Never. It was hard enough to feed a family of nine on a pastor's salary."

"But I bet you were never bored, huh?" He stepped over another fallen tree and helped Allie.

"True. And there was never a quiet moment, privacy, or vacations to Disneyland."

"I dunno. If I had to pick between Disney and having a house full of kids, I know what I'd pick."

Allie stilled. "You want a big family?"

"Oh yeah. I hated growing up alone. I mean, it was probably for the best, but…I always wanted brothers and sisters. So hopefully, when I get married, we can have a house full. At least four or five."

She didn't return his grin. Maybe this hadn't been such a good idea. Was he scaring her talking about marriage and kids? Didn't girls like guys that wanted that kind of stuff?

Smoke in the distance caught his eye, just a thin wisp floating toward the sky. "There's the cabin. It didn't burn when the wildfire swept through here." Dakota pointed out a rocky retaining wall running along the back of the property.

Allie stood next to him. "How is that possible?"

"Between that wall and the creek running along the side, the backyard is pretty clear of trees. It was enough of a break to funnel the fire that way toward the road we used to escape."

"Hey, there's a truck over there. Look. It's under the tarp."

"Someone might be here then. We should—"

A gunshot broke through the silence of the forest.

Dakota slammed into Allie and tackled her to the ground.

Ooof. "Was that—"

"Dunno." He got up but pushed her behind the wide trunk of a burnt spruce tree. "Stay here." He swung off his pack and dug through it.

"Where are you going?"

Dakota pulled out binoculars. "I can't see anything, but we need to get out of here."

"Maybe they don't know we're out here. It could've been an accident."

"I don't think I want to stick around and find out. You?"

"What do we do?" Allie's wide eyes looked to him.

He quickly scanned the area with the glasses. Lowered them. "I don't see anyone. But when I tell you, run that way. We'll follow the creek. Stay low and move from tree to tree. Ready?"

Her hands trembled a little, but she gave him a firm nod.

"Let's move." They ran to the next tree.

Another shot sounded.

So much for hoping it'd been a fluke. Someone was definitely trying to kill them.

Good thing Dakota didn't go anywhere unarmed. He pulled out his SIG Sauer and checked his mag. All set. He pulled out a small mirror and used it to check behind him. He couldn't see the shooter. He'd have to draw him out.

He couldn't just shoot the man. Not without proof. Even though everything inside said this *was* the dangerous man who'd murdered Paulson, that wouldn't fly in court. Dakota had to be sure. He used his phone and zoomed in on the cabin.

A face appeared in one of the small windows on the east side. Dakota snapped the photo and ducked back behind the tree. He couldn't see the hair or tattoo, but the shot of the man's face was pretty clear.

If nothing else, they could at least identify who this guy was later if they needed to tell the sheriff or someone who they'd seen.

He whispered to Allie. "I'm going to lay some cover. When I say go, you run as fast as you can."

She looked over at him with trust and determination. First date in the woods, covered in dirt because he'd tackled her to the ground, and now they were in a gunfight? Some kind of party, but he'd have preferred to take her to dinner.

Then again, if she could handle this, she could handle anything.

"Go."

He swung around the burnt tree trunk and fired in the air above the log cabin. Allie sprinted away. Movement flashed again in the same window, only this time the window was open. Another shot fired. A chunk of bark high above Dakota's head fell.

Good. If the shooter stayed aimed at him, it gave Allie the best chance at getting away. Dakota shot again, aiming above the window. He ran opposite of Allie to another wide tree. He ducked low and shot four more times.

No more shots sounded from the cabin, but a door slammed shut. Heavy footsteps pounded on gravel. Dakota had the higher ground, but if the guy went after Allie, she would be defenseless.

He ducked low and glanced around the tree but couldn't see anyone. Whoever this shooter was, he was definitely out there. Better save the ammo and cover Allie's escape.

He dodged from tree trunk to rock outcropping to tree. He spotted Allie racing downhill, parallel to the creek like he'd said. The creek had to lead to the river cutting through the forest. He sprinted to catch up with her, using the hill for coverage.

His pulse was too loud to hear anything else.

Lord, protect us. Help me keep her safe.

He glanced behind them enough to finally catch a good look at the man. Tall, a long, dingy ponytail, camo cargo pants and black shirt. He held a rifle and took aim. Dakota ran.

A shot fired again, hitting the ground somewhere behind him. The man was on their trail.

Allie slowed down to look over her shoulder at him.

He waved her on. "Run! Don't stop." He kept right behind her.

Their best option was to put more distance and obstacles between them and the shooter. He would have to decide if he would pursue or stop and take aim. Dakota weaved around the trees in their path. The slope helped them move fast, but it would give their pursuer the height advantage.

Another shot cracked the air. It hit far to Dakota's left.

Let the man waste his ammo.

We need a way out of here. If this guy had spent any amount of time in these woods, he knew them better than Allie and Dakota did.

Their best bet at getting away might be the river.

Branches whooshed past his face as he ran. Ash and smoke still rose from the blackened trees around them until he had to fight for breath and cough out the dirt.

Each step sent a fine gray dust into the air. Maybe Dakota could use that to obscure the man's sight. He scuffed his feet a few steps, making plumes of dust clouds.

Heavy footfalls behind them didn't slow.

The shooter was gaining on them.

Up ahead the slope grew steeper. Allie hit a patch of loose dirt. She listed sideways and started to slide downhill.

Dakota reached down and grabbed her arm, helping her back up.

"Thanks," she said, her voice breathy.

Dakota glanced back but couldn't see the shooter. He held his gun ready—just in case. In front of them, the creek flowed between two boulders in a huge wall formation that blocked their way. So much for following the creek to the river.

"Where do we go?" Allie wiped hair out of her face and sucked in air.

"We have to keep moving." He helped her up and over the rocks. If they couldn't make distance count, they needed coverage. They climbed down from the boulders and found a deer path on the other side.

"Let's go." He held her hand as they continued running. "Maybe we'll lose him."

"I…hope…so…I can't…run much farther."

But she continued to jog a decent pace with him. Here the trees were green again, the forest pristine. *Thank You.* The green provided extra foliage and cover as they ran.

The sound of falling rocks behind them meant the stranger was making his way through the boulders too, right on their tail. Dakota found a burst of speed.

Suddenly the path ended. Huge spruce and pine blocked their way. But there was open area beyond them and the sound of rushing water. They had to be close to the river. Dakota pushed through the fringe of branches and froze.

Pebbles fell down the cliff wall in front of him and dropped into the raging river over twenty feet below.

"Stop, Allie!" He grabbed her just as she was about to run through the tree branches and off the face of the mountain.

She gasped. He held her against himself while she found her bearings.

"What are we going to do?" She clung to his shirt, her hazel eyes wide.

"There's no way back."

Allie leaned over the cliff edge.

"We don't have time to debate this." Even now, footfalls were moving toward them, slightly drowned out by the sound of the river. A wild river, deep from the spring runoff, rushed down the mountain in a wide stream of tumbling white water. "We have to jump."

She shook her head.

"Allie." He squeezed her hand. "This is our only chance. I need you to jump as far out as you can. Once you hit the water, keep your feet in front of you and let the river take you downstream. I'll find you."

A fierce barking sounded on the wind.

"That's Scout!" Allie whipped around, looking for her dog.

Noise on the path behind the trees grew louder. The shooter was close.

Dakota released her hand. Turned to cover her. "You have to jump. Now!"

With one last look at him, Allie clenched her jaw tight. She closed her eyes and leaped. Her scream echoed off the canyon walls.

TEN

THE ARCTIC WATER STOLE ALLIE'S BREATH AS THE rapids dragged her downstream. *Dakota!*

She swam to the surface just in time to see Dakota jump off the cliff. She fought the current to see him splash down into the river.

He'd waited for her, made sure she was safe yet again.

Something dark on the cliff edge above her caught her eye. A dog barked. A reflective orange collar practically glowed against his black fur. It *was* Scout!

Before she could call to him, a man with a ponytail broke through the trees above them. He held out a gun, pointed at Dakota.

She screamed.

The gunman spotted her, but the river sucked her back under.

Allie fought against the ice-cold water. The weight of her clothes and backpack dragged her down. She kicked hard, trying to surface again, and managed to catch another breath.

It wasn't enough.

The water pulled her down once more.

She clawed at her backpack and tried to free herself of its burden. Her feet hit a hard surface—the bottom or another boulder. Didn't matter. She kicked off and broke through to the surface to see rocks and scrub brush passing by on the banks as she was carried along. Dakota had to be behind her somewhere, but it was all she could do to keep her head above the water and gulp in air.

Trees flew past in a blur. She finally got a few good breaths in.

Shore.

The cliff walls towered over her, but a thin strip of rocky shore gave her hope. She needed to aim for it. She pointed her feet toward the edge of the river, but the rapids spun her around. With heavy arms, she paddled enough to keep her head up.

There!

Up ahead, a fallen tree lay across the river, and beyond it a wider shoreline. The thick trunk dangled a foot or two in the air. If she could grab it, she could maybe hoist herself out of the water. At the very least, she could hold on and wait for Dakota. Maybe Scout would see her and come, and together they could make it to that clearing at the edge of the river.

She reached for the tree. Bark scraped against her hands. She fought the pain to grasp the lifeline. Dug her fingernails in. But the river carried her away under the log, submerging her as though all her efforts were nothing.

Allie tried to aim her beating strokes for the direction of the shoreline again only to be yanked under. Water thundered over her, pummeling her into its depths, filling her nose and mouth.

She kicked desperately. Her lungs burned with the need for oxygen. No! She couldn't go out this way. She had too much to make up for!

The more she fought, the weaker her arms grew. She couldn't breathe. Couldn't kick anymore. Her vision began to fade to black. Sounds muted to almost nothing.

Strong arms pulled her up and lifted her out of the water. She could've sworn she heard more barking, but it sounded far away. She coughed and gagged. Tried to catch her breath.

When she could finally open her eyes again, she found herself in Dakota's arms.

Somehow, he made it to a wide rocky shore. The river widened here, the water slowing to a gentle roll instead of the frothy white rapids. He carried her tight against his chest, his red hair plastered to his forehead, dripping water into his eyes. As soon as they were on dry land, he set her down.

"Allie?" He gasped air. "Please tell me you're okay." He coughed, leaned over, searching her face, pushing back her hair.

"I'm okay." Her raspy voice sounded weird even to her own ears. But she was alive.

She couldn't hold back the tears, and she buried her face in Dakota's chest.

He held her tight, chest heaving as he tried to catch his breath. "That was close."

Neither of them said anything for a few minutes.

Birds in the trees above them chirped and rustled. The gurgling river continued to traipse through the forest.

Allie took in each breath of fresh, pine-scented air

like the gift it was. Never again would she take breathing for granted.

Every breath we take is a gift from God.

Her father's words, not hers. But why did He keep saving her? She didn't deserve this gift. She didn't deserve any of it. She'd lost—wait! *Scout.*

Allie twisted around to scan the cliff. "I saw him. I saw Scout. Where is he?"

"I heard him, but I can't see him anywhere." Dakota stood up. "I don't know how far the river carried us, but that guy is still out there. Do you think you can stand?"

She nodded. He helped her to her feet, not letting go of her hands. Everything tilted around her. Allie leaned too far over, trying to compensate. Dakota wrapped an arm around her waist.

"Whoa, there. Take your time." Once she stopped swaying, he moved to hold her arms. He steadied her with his solid strength.

She shook water out of her ears and was able to catch her balance. "I think I've got it."

"You sure?"

"Yeah." She took a few shaky steps.

Dakota held her hand. "Good, cuz we need to get out of here."

Allie stopped, squeezed the hand he gave her. "We can't go yet. We have to find Scout."

"The shooter is after us. We can't go back."

"We can't leave my dog out here on his own."

"Allie, I know we need to find him, but we'll have to come back later. Besides, this is good news. We saw him. We know he's okay. And we already know that he can find us. But right now, we have to keep going."

But they were so close. He was here, somewhere in the forest. Lost and alone. "How can I leave him?" Her voice cracked. She couldn't turn her back on him when she'd promised herself. "I can't do it. You can go on."

"Allie." Dakota shook her gently, his bright blue eyes intense, worried as he stared at her. "We have to get back and show the sheriff who this guy is. If he's the guy Ethan and Nolan saw, then he's killed an Army Ranger. He knows we saw him. He'll be coming after us, and he might be after the boys. We have to go. Do you understand?"

She tried spinning around, desperate for any glimpse of the dark black fur. "I already lost a baby. I can't walk away. Not when he's so close. Scout needs me." Dizziness stole all balance. Allie fell against Dakota.

"Baby? You mean, Dixie? Like a fur baby?"

She'd said *baby*? She hadn't meant—

She pushed Dakota away and stood straight, bracing herself as she fought the dizziness. "Nothing. I—it was nothing. You're right. We have to go." The seal was breaking. She'd escaped one near drowning. This wasn't the time for another. Because as soon as the dam holding back the past broke, there would be no coming up to the surface for breath. She wouldn't make it.

"Are you sure you—"

"I'm okay, Dakota. Let's go." She swallowed down the sob trying to choke her.

The sopping wet clothes and shoes weighed on her body, but as they picked their way around the rocks along the river, she slowly gained her strength back. She stopped to cough a few times, but they would wait until she caught her breath, then push on. Always pushing on. The farther they went, the deeper she pushed back the memories.

Dakota's gaze drifted to her constantly. She tried to pick up the pace, convince him that she wasn't about to fall apart.

"Hey, what's that?" Allie spotted purple fabric up ahead along the water. "My backpack!" It was there, caught in the branches of an overturned tree. Nothing edible remained, but the water bottles were salvageable, and it still had Scout's favorite toy and some gear that she would've had to replace had it been lost.

She pulled out the baggie. "We still have the bandana."

Dakota nodded. "All we need now is a way out."

"Right. Let's keep going." Everything was wet and smelly. But that man, the shooter, was out there in the forest, and so was her dog. And somehow, she needed to come back here and find Scout and then leave. Quickly.

Kinda the story of her life. Always running. Never finding that haven she searched for.

Either way, there was nothing else here for her but to keep moving.

Dakota had no idea what had happened to Allie there by the river, but something was broken between them, and he didn't know how to fix it.

Allie had kinda fallen apart and then pushed him away. Wouldn't most people be grateful after being saved from drowning? Was she that upset that they hadn't gone back for Scout?

She wouldn't look at him at all once that rafting party had found them and taken them back to the campground. She'd only spoken to him when she'd asked him to drive her car. And there she sat, head slumped against the passenger side window, eyes slammed shut. But with every bump in the road, she winced, so she must not be sleeping. What was going on?

Lord, if I can help here, You'll have to guide me. But more than anything, I know Allie needs Your healing touch.

He just didn't know why. But he had some suspicions. Lots of people called their pets their children, but—

"So..." He kept his voice soft. "Baby?"

"I don't want to talk about it." Her clipped words echoed off the window she faced.

Whoa-kay then. After all they'd been through, she still didn't trust him. He shouldn't be surprised. It wasn't like they'd known each other long, but he really thought they'd connected. He'd actually seen a future with Allie.

Guess once again, he was wrong.

He glanced at her. Dripping hair, damp clothes, and shivering despite the soaring temps outside. Like it or not, it tugged at his heart. "Let's swing by your place and grab you a change of clothes. We can shower and change at base camp and then head to the sheriff's office. If you still want to."

"We should go to the sheriff first." She didn't lift her head from the window.

"You need a hot shower and dry clothes. The sheriff can wait. Besides, maybe he'll take us a little more seriously if we don't show up looking like drowned rats."

"I suppose." Allie laid her head back on the seat and closed her eyes.

Rest was probably the best thing for her.

Thankfully, base camp was quiet, the parking lot mostly empty with most of the crew out enjoying the reprieve of a day off. They showered, changed quickly, and—after redoing his bandages, this time by himself—they got back in Allie's SUV. He tried not to bother her with chitchat while she drove.

As soon as they entered the sheriff's office, he spotted Ray Haroldson behind bars in the small holding cell. Dakota tried to quench the desire to knock the arrogant smirk right off his face. But being surrounded by desks, three other deputies in uniform, and a woman answering phones kept him in check. The smell of ink, coffee, and stress, and the beeping and scratchy voices on the radios had a calming effect, reminding him of his SWAT days with his own team back in Benson.

The sheriff sighed as they walked in the door. "Let me guess. You're here as two concerned citizens again to give me intel on my open murder case?"

Dakota told him about their morning. Allie sat there, saying nothing. It was almost like the light in her had been snuffed out.

"Allie, can you show him what we found?"

"Hmm?"

He nodded to her bag.

"Oh, right. We found this." Allie pulled out the soggy baggie with the bandana.

That was it? Didn't she have more to say?

The sheriff studied the bag.

"And we can give you a description of the shooter in the woods," Dakota said. "He was tall, six-four or six-five, and had dark hair pulled back in a long ponytail, but he was balding on top. He had the tattoo of a gun and a flag running up his right arm." Dakota pointed to his computer. "I even took a picture of his face and emailed it to you."

Hutchinson pecked at his keyboard and stared at his screen. With a long sigh he leaned back in his chair and ran his hands down his face. "That's Earl Blackwell."

"So, you know him?" Dakota asked.

"He and his brother are usually up to no good, but they're smart enough to cover their tracks. We don't have enough evidence to do anything. Besides, the feds are storming in. They want a piece of the action since the victim was a Ranger."

"But you have two kids who witnessed a murder, and that makes them loose ends to tie up. And this Earl was shooting at us. We'll testify." Dakota tried to keep the irritation out of his voice.

"I'll go out to his cabin and some of the places he's been known to hang out, but I guarantee you, even if we could find him—and that's a big if, since he was born and raised in that forest—he would come up with some valid excuse. He could claim you were trespassing, thought you were an intruder, or any number of reasons for shooting at you. And his brother would back him up."

Allie sat straight in her chair. "So you're just going to let him get away with this? You can run forensics on the bandana."

There she was, finally coming out of whatever funk she'd been in.

"And you have two eyewitnesses. Ethan and Nolan. They'll need protection." Dakota would do it himself if need be.

"I tried talking to the boys, but Jen refused to let me. She also refused to tell me how she was injured or anything about the fire."

"And you just dropped it?" Dakota tried not to sound accusing, but come on.

"I'm not giving up on anything, but I told you already, leave the investigating to me. You two could've gotten killed out there."

Dakota almost jumped from his seat. "But we didn't. We can help."

"You wanna help? Go do your job. Protect this town from the fire that's out of control on that mountain. I don't need any more victims."

"And what are you going to do?"

"Not that it's any of your business, but I will personally track down Earl. You, however, need to stay out of it. You don't want to mess with those Blackwell brothers. Their father was Russian military. They're dangerous. So please do us all a favor and stick to firefighting. Let me do my job."

Good thing danger didn't scare him, then. But obviously, they weren't going to get any further here. And the sad stare in Allie's eyes was back. Was she even paying attention, picking at the loose strings from her cutoffs?

"Let's go, Allie."

They ignored Ray as they walked past the holding cell and all the others in the open office area. They stepped out into the hazy sunshine, but he couldn't keep going like this. As soon as they hit the sidewalk, he grabbed her hand and pulled her aside.

"Hey, are you okay?"

Her eyes filled, but for the first time since the river rescue, she really looked at him.

"Please, Allie. Talk to me. What did I do?"

One tear fell to her cheek before she wiped it away. "It's not about you, Dakota. And...I just can't. This is my problem. Not yours."

"C'mon. I'll feed you. Will that help? You've got to be starving."

"Maybe." She gave him a half-hearted smile. "But I'd rather get a new phone. What if someone tries calling about Scout?"

He might not be able to fix everything, but he could at least get her set up with a new cell and feed her. He could be a safe place for her. Maybe then she'd admit what was really eating her up inside.

They stopped for the replacement phones and found a little Mexican restaurant not too far from the store. Within minutes they had a basket of warm chips and bowls of salsa in front of them.

Dakota dunked his chip in salsa and bit into it. The fresh flavors of tomato, onion, and cilantro reminded him of his favorite restaurant in Benson. He and the SWAT guys would often meet up there after a long day. "This is almost as good as Lucita's Taqueria back in Benson. I miss those enchiladas."

"I always liked the chimichangas there." Her dim smile didn't come close to convincing him that she was okay, but it was a start. "Why didn't you go back to Benson after rehab?"

Ah, back to deflecting, turning the questions on him. He'd play this for a while, but he'd been a decent cop for a lot of years. He knew when someone was hiding something.

"I dunno. Guess I wasn't quite ready to face everyone I let down. I was pretty messed up. Needed a new start."

"So where did you go when you finished at the Ridgeman Center?"

"I worked with a construction company called Workmen Not Ashamed. It's like a halfway house. They hire addicts and we live together, work together on building projects, and have a lot of accountability as we get our feet back under us again."

"Sounds like a really cool company. You didn't want to stay?"

"I always knew it was a temporary gig. The work, the Bible study, the crew leaders…it was all good. Maybe even necessary for a while. But I needed to see how I could handle life when I didn't have those accommodations. And because our room and board were included in this program, we didn't make a whole lot. So I figured a year was a good run and it was time to move on. One of the crew leaders was a hotshot and said they were hurting for workers this year and even offering a significant sign-on bonus for new hires that lasted the first ninety days. It will help me pay back Will for the rehab." He took a sip from his water. "What about you? What are you doing so far from home? There's lots of places closer to Benson you could train Scout."

"Yeah, but this was a good excuse to see Belle. We picked a park neither of us had been to, and I knew if it was closer to her place than mine, she would be more likely to come."

"Where does she live again?"

"Twin Valley, Idaho. Not too far from my parents, actually."

"Will you go see them, then, on your way back to Benson? Your family and Belle?"

"Maybe." She nibbled on a chip. "I'm sure they're all busy with their own lives."

"Are you trying to convince me or yourself?"

Her hand froze. "It's a fact. They all have jobs, families of their own—"

"When's the last time you saw them?"

"Belle's wedding last February."

"And before that?"

"What is this? Are you interrogating me or something?" Her chuckle fell flat.

He reached for her hand. It was still cold.

"Allie, I know something is bothering you. That breakdown by the river—"

"Don't make more out of it than it is. I almost drowned. My dog is still out there, lost, and there's a crazy man probably trying to kill us. If that's not reason for an emotional moment, then I don't know what is." She gulped down her own water.

"You said, 'I already lost a baby. I can't walk away.'"

Her body tensed and she tried to pull her hand out of his grip.

He didn't let her. He could wait her out all day if needed. Because with all the ways she'd supported him, cared for him, he wanted to do the same. To be a safe place for her to fall apart. To hold her together when that happened. But in order for them to have any future, she had to face this.

"I was talking about Scout." Her whisper was fraught with emotion as she tugged her hand free from his grip.

"You were pregnant, weren't you? With Christian's baby."

She shook her head. "I…" Her voice cracked. She looked away and swiped at the tears already spilling onto her cheek.

"You've never told anyone, have you? And whatever happened to that baby, it's tearing you up inside."

ELEVEN

THE WALLS CLOSED IN ON ALLIE. SHE HAD TO GET out of there. She pushed her way out of the booth, ran out of the restaurant.

"Allie, wait!"

She didn't look back, just ran. At the end of the block, she turned and headed to the river. There had to be somewhere she could be alone before she broke down completely. She must've lost Dakota.

Good. The nerve of that man saying out loud what she'd fought so hard to protect, to keep hidden. She should've left him as soon as they'd gotten back from the trail, but she wanted to see it through, to make sure Ethan and Nolan were going to be safe.

But she was the one in danger now.

She shouldn't have let down her guard with Dakota.

He was too astute. And just like before, in the car, he made her feel safe. And again, just like in the car, she was too easily falling for him.

Well, now she'd probably scared him away for good. If he'd figured it out, he'd know to run far and fast *away* from her. She slowed down to a jog. Her lungs seized as a coughing fit overtook her, forcing her to stop completely by a bench on the riverfront to catch her breath.

Stupid smoke inhalation. The near drowning probably hadn't helped either. She collapsed on the bench and tried to take long, slow breaths.

"Allie!"

She looked up. Dakota jogged toward her. Great. He'd found her. And she had nowhere else to go. Betrayed by her own body. Again.

He rushed over and grabbed her hands once more. She had no more strength to pull away physically.

But she could push him away with the truth.

"Go away, Dakota. You don't need to do anything. I'm fine."

"You're not fine. Not by a long shot."

"I will be. Just..." She wanted to say *Take me home*. But home was far away. And Scout was still here. And...everything she'd worked so hard at constructing was tumbling down all around her.

She watched the river water swirl and flow past them.

Dakota sat next to her, wrapped her in his strong arms, her head tucked under his chin. "I'm not going anywhere, Al. I don't know what it is, but I'm here. I'll keep knocking on this door until you let me in."

"That's what I'm afraid of."

"Huh?"

"Kota, you deserve so much better." She'd already come to terms with her condition. She couldn't impose it on him.

"Are you kidding? You know where I've been. What I am—"

"Yeah, but—"

His words came back from earlier in the day.

I hated growing up alone. I mean, it was probably for the best, but...I always wanted brothers and sisters. So hopefully, when I get married, we can have a houseful. At least four or five.

"You want a big family."

One brow rose. "And that's bad?"

Yes, it was. Because even though she knew there was no hope for them, he was the kind of guy who would try, and it wasn't fair to steal all his hopes for a good future. And the only thing that would probably convince him to leave her in peace was the stark-naked truth.

"You need to find someone else, Dakota."

He smiled one of those smiles that brought out his dimples. He tenderly swept a lock of hair behind her ear. "You're not getting rid of me that easily. You saw me at my worst, and you still gave me a chance. I'm willing to do the same. So you fell for a jerk of a guy, got pregnant. My own romantic past isn't squeaky clean by a long shot. But I think we still have something here. We could—"

"No, we can't, Dakota." She pushed him away and stood. "I didn't just get pregnant. I got an abortion. An abortion that wasn't under the most sanitary of conditions. I was so stupid and desperate for a man who didn't love me that I sacrificed my own child. Not only that, but the ability to have *any* children, because my uterus became so infected I needed a hysterectomy. Now do you see why there's no future here?" She pointed to the empty space between them.

Her voice had gotten loud, but Dakota stayed silent.

He didn't have to say anything. The pain in his eyes was enough. The smile fell. The dimples faded away. His brows furrowed together. Finally, he was getting the message.

"So you see, I'll be paying for the rest of my life for that choice, for getting caught up in a fantasy. This is why I need to find Scout. Search and rescue gives me a chance at trying to make up for it all. And this is why you should just forget any idea of there being an 'us.' I deserve what I have. You deserve so much more."

Her voice cracked, but she lifted her chin. She needed a strong front here. One he wouldn't try to knock down. Because if anyone could, if anyone were stubborn enough, it would probably be Dakota Masterson who could find the weakness in her walls and bore through to the tender core of her heart only to be disappointed with what he found inside. And she couldn't bear the thought of that.

Christian's rejection had literally almost killed her. So it was better this way.

"We're not far from the base. If you don't mind bringing my car back, I'm going to walk." She turned and walked away.

"So, you're leaving?" He ran up to her.

"It's for the best." She kept walking.

But Dakota put himself in the middle of her path. "This is why you've pushed everyone out of your life, won't answer your father's calls. Won't let anyone close. To punish yourself? This is why you're hiding?"

"Like you're not hiding yourself? You're not exactly an open book about your addiction with the team. I thought if anyone could understand, it would be you."

"We're talking about people I've barely met. You haven't told your own family or best friend."

"Maybe I wanted a blank slate too." She thumped her chest with a fist. "But don't you get it? Mine will *never* be wiped clean. I have to live with the consequences for the rest of my life. Every time I watch one of my siblings or friends get married, have kids, I die a little knowing I will never have that. And you can say now that you'll love me through it all, or it doesn't matter because we'll have each other, but I've heard that before. I can't fall for it again."

"I'm not gonna lie and say it doesn't matter at all to me, but you never even gave me the chance. But why don't you, right now? Stay here. Fight for this. For us."

For a moment she was tempted. That earnestness sparking in his eyes, the firm hold he had on her hand, drew her in. Again she found herself clinging to his strength. Maybe Dakota really would be the kind of man who could overlook it all. But for how long?

It might hurt him now, but the honest to goodness truth was that he deserved so much more than she could give. He would see that eventually.

"Good intentions aren't enough. This is one fight you can't win." No one could.

This time when she walked away, he didn't come after her.

And that was for the best.

He shouldn't be surprised that another person was walking out of his life. But the pain that hit him the moment Allie turned away almost brought him to his knees. How had he let it get this far so fast? His first instinct was to run after her, but he quickly doused it.

So what that she was the first person he'd ever opened up to and shared his past with. The ugly parts and all. Or that she was the kind of woman who'd seen him at his worst, the open gaping wounds, and stepped forward to help bandage him up. Maybe she was simply a good nurse and he'd read way too much into it.

He'd thought she'd be the kind of woman who could handle the messiness of life and not be scared away. Guess he was wrong. He'd tried. If she didn't want to fight for him, who was he to try to convince her otherwise?

Since he had her keys, he drove her car and parked it at base headquarters. He walked up to the big open bay where the trucks were. No one was there, but a back door opened to the concrete pad behind the building. The whole hotshot and smokejumper crew was present, a couple guys at the grill flipping burgers, the others sitting in camping chairs, on coolers, or at the one picnic table set up.

Houston waved him over. "Hey, where have you been? I haven't been able to get ahold of you."

"Sorry, my phone was ruined."

"How'd you do that? Drop it or something?"

"Not exactly." He went on to tell Houston about Earl and their chase through the forest and river escape. The others quieted, listening in on the story.

Alex Sheehy whistled. "Dude, you got some crazy death wish?" He chuckled. "First you go running into a forest on fire, a tree almost falls on you while you're on the line, and now some guy is trying to shoot you and you almost drown?"

"A man died out there in the mountains. An Army Ranger. He deserves justice. Answers. And there are two little boys who are caught up in the middle of it. They need protection."

"Are you talking about the body they found? The guy was a Ranger?" Kane asked. "How do you know?"

"I talked with the ME. He's been identified as Kurt Paulson." Dakota reached into a cooler and grabbed a can.

"What's an Army Ranger doing in the middle of Nowheresville with the likes of this hick? What's his name? Earl?" Logan, one of the smokejumpers, asked.

"That's what I'd like to know." Dakota shut the lid to the cooler.

Eric Dale wiggled his fingers in the air. "Maybe he wasn't really a Ranger. Maybe he's a spook."

"CIA? Yeah, right. That's just you and your crazy conspiracy theories talking again, Dale," Charlie Benning said.

The others laughed.

Ramos spoke up. "There's nothing out here. It's miles and miles of forest and mountain."

"Yeah, think about it. A great place to hide if that's what ya need to do." Unlike the others, Booth wasn't joking around.

"I don't know about you, but I'll stick to fighting fires." Emily and Jojo, sitting next to each other, bumped fists.

"What are you going to do, Dakota?" Booth asked.

He popped open his can. "Not sure."

The conversation switched to baseball. Dakota

slipped away without notice and looked out over the mountains. It was hard to distinguish the clouds from the smoke and haze.

What am I supposed to do? The sheriff says stay out of it. Allie doesn't want to be a part of anything. So, God, why did You bring her back into my life if I was just going to screw it up?

She wasn't wrong. He was trying to hide his past too, afraid of what this team would think. It was part of his story. But if he was adamant that she should get her own past out in the open, he should probably be more forthcoming about his own.

Miles Dafoe came out of the building. "Troops, let's round up. We've got a callout."

"Aw, it's our day off, Commander. I thought that team from California was on call today," someone around the grill said. Probably Orion.

"Fire doesn't care. The wind picked up, and they need our help to push it east toward the river. Let's head out."

Dakota ran inside with the others to change and grab his gear.

As they scrambled to load the truck and vans with the necessary equipment, Dafoe called out orders. "Masterson, you'll be working with Kane on the dig crew this time."

Probably, he didn't trust him with a chain saw, and he'd be better off avoiding any falling timber. Dakota gingerly felt his bandage through his shirt. Tried not to think of Allie nursing his wounds. This wasn't the time to worry about her.

"Saw Allie left before the barbecue ended." Kane nudged Dakota as they piled their water jugs into the back of the van.

"Yeah, so?"

"Everything okay? She seemed upset."

Dakota slammed the van door shut. "You wanna go comfort her? Go right ahead. But don't get too close unless you wanna get burned."

Kane lifted his hands in surrender fashion. "Whoa. Easy there. Not trying to move in on your girl."

"She's made her decision when it comes to me." Dakota grabbed his pack.

Houston looked over at them as he walked to the front passenger seat. "Really? So you're just going to give up?"

"Allie made her choice."

"And what choice was that?" Houston asked.

"To walk away. And believe me, I gave her plenty of chances to stay." Dakota moved to get in the van.

Kane stopped him with a heavy hand on his shoulder. "I don't know why you're letting a woman like Allie get away. You fight for everything else. Why not her?"

"She doesn't want me. Or at least, she's not willing to stay and try to figure something out. What more do you want me to do? Beg?"

"If that's what it takes, yes." Kane looked at him like the answer was obvious. Houston just shrugged.

"She knows about my past. About me." And maybe, like his mother, what she saw wasn't enough. Goodness knows she'd seen enough instances of him acting exactly like his father.

"What are you talkin' about?" Orion asked as he walked up.

"I have a temper. It can cause a lot of trouble. And—" He might as well tell them. "I'm an addict.

Got kicked off my last team for good reason. I put them at risk. So maybe she's the smart one to walk away."

"You really believe that? 'Cause if you're talking about taking down that drunk who beat up his wife, I don't think anyone here would fault you for it." Kane looked around at the others gathered by the van as he said it. Sax shook his head a little. Houston simply shrugged. Charlie almost looked bored.

Nobody seemed particularly upset or horrified about his admission.

Maybe they didn't understand. "That's part of it. But…it's also bad genetics too. My old man…well, let's just say he didn't particularly need a reason for a good beatdown."

"That doesn't mean you're bound to be the same." Houston plopped his pack in his seat.

"But I *am* the same. I fought my own brother. And he was just trying to help me."

"Help you how?" Charlie asked.

"He was the one that told me I needed help. I didn't take it very well. I could blame it on the oxycodone-induced haze, but the truth is I was just really messed up and Will made a convenient target."

"You beat him up?" Hammer asked.

"Psh. Yeah, right. I got one solid hit. Will took it easy on me, but I still landed flat on my back." As soon as his head had cleared enough to realize what he'd done, he'd been eaten up with remorse, but it was too late. The damage had been done. Dani had helped him to his feet, his nose bleeding. The twins had stared at him like he'd torn every shred of faith they had in him. Will had just stared at him, jaw taut, eyes filled with something like pity.

"I don't know if I've ever known such shame." Dakota's voice dropped to almost nothing.

"So that's the regret you carry around." Kane said it like he might actually understand.

Dakota didn't say anything. Of course he carried that regret around.

He might've kicked the pill-popping habit, but nothing was going to cure him of being that hotheaded kid. He was Buck Masterson's son, after all. So Allie was smart to leave now, before he dragged her down further.

"Look, we all have a past. But I see you studying that Bible before you go to sleep at night. Isn't there something about forgiveness in there, Houston? You're a pastor, right?" Kane asked.

Dakota knew all the verses. "Yeah, I know I'm forgiven but…I dunno. I've got a lot to make up for. I want to be a better example for my nephews, prove to my brother that all that he's invested in me isn't a waste. To show God that I'm grateful. And to show people that I'm nothing like my father."

"Maybe you're so busy trying to prove something that you've forgotten who your heavenly Father is. He fought for you. Chose you. And all your sin, not just some of it, has been paid for and taken away. Instead of trying so hard to pay back the grace you've been given, why don't you simply receive it for the gift it is?"

Houston's words landed with an impact.

Was that what Dakota was doing? Trying to earn the grace of God? Because, yes, it felt very much like it was up to him to prove to the world he was more like his heavenly Father than his earthly one.

"And about Allie?" Kane spoke up. "You're an idiot. You like her. You should fight for her."

"What do you know about it?"

"I know a little about how regret can erode a man from the inside. How finding a good woman, a brave woman, a woman who sees something inside a guy like me, is a rare gift. And I know this because I was an idiot too. I let the woman I love slip away. You still have time to make this right with Allie."

"She left."

"Tell me, is she leaving because she doesn't like you, or is she leaving because she's scared?"

"I thought she liked me. But…she's got her own past she's grappling with."

"Then she's probably running away. Don't let her. Tell her you'll wait."

"It's not that easy. I don't have a car."

"You can take my truck when we get back. I'm driving it to the site. See you in a bit." He strode away to his black Silverado.

Maybe Kane was right. Maybe his knee-jerk reaction was pushing her away mostly to protect himself.

But before he could do anything, they had a fire to put out.

TWELVE

ALLIE SLAPPED THE FRESHLY PRINTED PAPER WITH Scout's picture on the telephone pole and stapled it down.

She released a shuddery breath. With one hand, she reached for a tissue in her pocket and wiped her nose. But rather than drying up the tears, the farther Allie walked down the sidewalk in town, the worse they got.

Her phone rang. Oh, she was such a fool for hoping it was him. She jammed the papers and stapler in the messenger bag and pulled out her new cell.

Nope. Belle.

Allie cleared her throat and answered it.

"Hey." Hopefully the false cheer would throw her off the scent.

"Any news about Scout?"

Allie focused on the western-style lettering of the thrift store across the street. "I saw him. He's alive, but he ran off, and a crazy man named Earl was shooting at us, so—"

"Say what?!"

She walked to the next pole and stapled another

poster while she told Belle everything that had happened in the woods.

Almost everything. No need to share the details about kissing Dakota or her emotional breakdown.

"Allie, what's wrong?"

Shoot. Shoulda known Belle would pick up on her internal distress.

"I'm fine. Just...worried about Scout." Hopefully Belle would leave it at that.

But the silence on the line did not bode well. Even from a couple hundred miles away, her best friend was reading her.

"Allison Jane Monroe. What's going on? What happened with Dakota?"

"Why do you think something happened with Dakota? I lost my dog. I almost drowned. Obviously that's been very upsetting." She slammed the palm of her hand against the stapler harder than necessary.

"Because I haven't heard this kind of heartbreak in your voice since that jerk Christian left you."

"It's that obvious, huh?" Her throat tightened, making it hard to swallow.

"We've known each other since the church nursery. Spill it. What did he do to you?"

The tears started in earnest. "He didn't do anything, Belle. It's me. I'm the problem." She turned the corner and walked toward her vehicle, keeping her head down.

"You're not a problem! How can you say that?"

"Because I'm the one doing the leaving this time. Dakota deserves someone better. I should've never let it get as far as I did. There was never any future there."

"Why the heck not? He's a real-life hero. He saved your life. Twice."

"I know. That's why he deserves someone else. No matter how much he thinks he's falling for me—"

"He said that?"

Allie sighed. She reached her car and sat behind the wheel. "Yeah. He asked me to give him a chance."

"Then for goodness' sake, give the man a chance. What more are you waiting for?"

"I told you. Marriage is not my calling—"

"You never once told me why though. When we were kids, all we talked about was growing up and getting married. Having *our* kids in the church nursery together. So you're gonna tell me that one guy breaks your heart and you're going to give up on it all?"

"It's more complicated than that." Allie traced the stitching on her steering wheel. Too bad her own life wasn't so nice and neat. Everything lined up the way it should be.

"Then explain it to me. Because I know there was a lot more that went on with Christian than you're telling me. I've never pushed, but maybe I should've. Because you've never been the same since. What really happened?"

She'd already been through it once. Maybe that was how Belle's quiet question broke the dam. Or maybe she was simply tired of carrying it all. Either way, Allie allowed the whole story to come out.

And afterwards, she endured the long, painful silence, half expecting Belle to hang up.

Then, "Have you been punishing yourself this whole time? Thinking it was all your fault?"

Allie couldn't answer. Too much emotion squeezed

her throat, cutting off words. Salty tears ran down her face.

"Oh, Allie." Belle sniffed. "And what? You think God punished you by taking away your ability to have children?"

Well, yeah. That's exactly what she thought. She'd disobeyed, and sin had consequences.

"By your silence, I guess the answer is yes." Belle paused. "Allie, I want you to listen to me carefully. We don't always have answers for the way or why things happen. But know this: God's forgiveness is complete. He's not punishing you. Remember that hymn? 'My sin, not in part but the whole, is nailed to the cross, and I bear it no more.'"

The melody ran through her mind.

Praise the Lord, praise the Lord, O my soul.

It had been a long time since Allie had felt like praising the Lord. Somewhere along the line, she'd stopped going to church. Every time she walked in the doors, she felt like an imposter. She didn't belong.

Belle's voice broke through her thoughts. "You've carried this burden too long. And you were never meant to."

"I knew what I was doing, Belle. I lied to you. Lied to my family. How can you even stand to speak to me right now?"

"Mostly, I think you lied to yourself, Al, by thinking you deserve what you got. But there's grace. Mercy. Loving kindness. Did you forget about those? Did you really think I'd reject you and all our years of friendship because you messed up?"

Maybe. Because those always seemed like things other people deserved. Not her.

"Forgiveness and mercy can never be earned.

Because there's only one person good enough to pay the debt for all our sin. Only one who could bear that burden. I love you, but it's not you. And if Dakota is someone who has opened up your heart to start living again, if he's heard all this and still wants a shot, maybe don't write him off quite yet."

Maybe she had a point.

"I'll think about it." A beep sounded on her phone. "I gotta go. I'm getting another call."

"Okay, but, Al, I think Dakota is right. I think you should tell your parents. They've been worried about you too. You're long overdue for a visit."

"I know. I'll talk to you soon."

She pressed the icon to answer the other call. It was a local number.

Allie answered it quickly. "Hello?"

"It's Ray."

Ray? Why would he be calling her? "Where's Jen? Are the boys okay?"

"I found your dog."

"You have Scout?"

"I was driving out by the campground and saw him. He's here." His voice sounded different.

"How did you get this number?"

"It's on his collar. Now, do you want the mutt or not? I don't have all night."

"Don't go anywhere. I'm on my way."

"You'll have that reward too?"

"I'm not giving you a cent until I see my dog, and if there's even a scratch on him, you can forget it."

"Then you better come get him. I could use the money."

"I'm on my way."

He might not be Dixie, but Scout was her dog, and she wanted him back at her side.

"Can't this go any faster?" Dakota tried to keep the grumble out of his voice. He checked his phone again while they took a short water break from cutting down fuel to help funnel the fire toward the river. Still no reception.

Kane glanced over at him. "Impatient, are we?"

With this feeling in his gut? More like he felt like something had gone very, very wrong. His phone chimed.

He moved uphill and checked again. Finally! A voicemail from Allie.

Hey, if you get this, will you call me back? I need to talk to you. But Ray called. He found Scout out at the campground. I'm not crazy about seeing him out there alone, but I can't wait. I know I don't have the right to ask anything of you, but could you meet me out there?

Dakota checked the time of the call. Over an hour ago.

"Shoot."

"What's wrong?" Kane asked.

"Allie went to meet up with Ray. By herself."

"Why would she do that?" Hammer asked.

"He says he found Scout out at the campground." Dakota called her. Maybe she'd waited and he could convince her to hold off until he could go with her. "Hey, Allie."

"Listen up, hotshot."

Dakota's blood ran cold at the unmistakable voice. "Ray." He didn't bother masking his own fury.

"What are you doing with Allie's phone? Where is she?"

"So, you do care what happens to the girl. Good."

Ray was out of jail, and he had Allie. *God, don't let this be what I think it is.*

Dakota shushed everyone up and put the call on speaker.

"Listen up," Ray said. "If you want to see her alive, you'll come alone to the campground. And before you get any bright ideas, you should know I've got friends. One is keeping an eye on the boys. I know they're with Jen's sister. If I see you come with anyone else, they know what to do with them, and no one will find their bodies. If you call the cops, I happen to have a friend there too. I'll know. And Jen will lose them both."

"Why are you doing this?"

"Because you talk too much. Especially to that sheriff. Earl isn't someone you want to cross, so if you wanna keep those brats and your girl safe, then you best get here real fast. And come alone."

The call ended before Dakota could demand more information. A feral growl ripped out of his throat. "He has Allie."

"Why is he doing this?" Houston asked.

Dakota wanted to drive a fist through something. "He's gotta have something going on with Earl Blackwell, some kind of deal that would tangle him up in the murder case."

"You can't go out there alone. He's probably bluffing about watching the boys." Orion wasn't joking around for once.

"Would you be willing to take that chance?" Dakota stared him down.

Bottom line, Ray wanted out—of Ember and everything else—and he was using Allie as bait.

Kane's jaw clenched. "Fine. You can use my truck. And we're putting a tracker of some sort on you. Ham and I can secure and safeguard the boys in town while you get Allie."

"Thanks." The word wasn't sufficient, but it was all he could squeeze out.

Through the rage at the injustice of it all, to have innocent people in the grasp of a man like Ray, it helped to have someone like Kane watching his back. It had been a while since he'd had that. Almost like they were a team again, like his SWAT brothers. If anything, admitting his addiction and his past had gained him the respect he'd been so certain they'd withhold. Instead, it'd fostered trust.

Dakota got in Kane's truck and drove north out of Ember toward the campground. The dark highway was eerily quiet. He pushed the needle past the speed limit, but the curvy switchbacks slowed him down as he made his way up the incline to the campground.

Lord, You hold not only the past but also the present and the future in Your hands. Guide me now. Protect Allie. Protect those boys. Let Your justice prevail tonight.

He was getting closer now. A billboard advertised the turn for the campgrounds, just a couple miles ahead. His stomach clenched tighter and tighter.

Hold on, Allie.

A pair of glowing green dots appeared in the ditch. Dakota slammed on the brakes, stopping just in time to miss the deer bounding out of the trees and into the road.

He kept his foot on the brake even after the deer crossed. Where there was one, there were often more.

He was about to get going again when another pair of eyes on the side of the road reflected in his headlights. This animal was shorter than the deer. With dark fur. Maybe a raccoon?

No. It approached the road and barked.

Dakota pulled the truck off the highway and jumped out. "Scout! Come here, boy."

The Lab came right to him, bounding around and licking Dakota's hands.

"What's going on. Why are you out here?" Ray was supposed to have him.

Scout whined. He barked and took a couple steps toward a trail coming out of the forest. It wasn't a groomed campground path—more of a deer trail. But he was acting like he wanted Dakota to follow him.

He barked again.

"All right, just a minute boy." Dakota rushed back to the truck.

Kane had tossed him the keys along with a comment that Dakota could use whatever he could find. Hopefully the guy had a heavy-duty flashlight he could use, maybe some emergency flares or something to use as a distraction.

He rifled through the center console. Nothing there. He flipped the front seat over. A black plastic case took up the width of the cab. Maybe Kane kept some emergency supplies there. Dakota opened it up.

"Whoa." What was Kane doing with a cache of guns and ammo in his truck?

Scout wiggled his nose between Dakota's hip and the open door.

Dakota wasn't sure he wanted to know what the guy was hiding.

For now, he grabbed a Glock 23 and extra clip, hoping the weapons weren't stolen.

In a duffel, he found a flashlight and a hunting knife in a sheath. He strapped the knife to his ankle and stuffed the light in the pocket of his cargo pants.

GPS on his phone indicated he wasn't that far from the campground. He'd follow Scout and see where the dog led him first. He shut the truck door. "Scout, find Allie."

He kept the flashlight off for now, trusting Scout to lead. There was enough moonlight filtering through the trees that it wasn't quite pitch black as they followed the narrow trail through the forest. His feet quickly climbed the slight incline of a trail winding through the forest.

A mile or so later, they reached the burnt area. Scout set a good trotting pace around the trees and rocks. Dakota jogged to keep up. From this direction, they would be heading in on the west side of the campground.

Dakota's plan was to take Ray by surprise if he was still there. But he'd still have to keep an eye out for any of Ray's watchdogs too. He didn't want to rush in if he was outnumbered, but he was going to save Allie.

God, help me save her.

Muffled voices carried on the wind.

Scout slowed. He whined but didn't bark. They must be getting close.

Dakota slowed his pace. They reached the top of a ridge, and he looked down. Somewhere in the middle of a stand of stately pines was a bright light—maybe a campfire.

Dakota strained to hear the voices better.

Definitely male. His gut said it was Ray. He had to get closer and see what he was walking into. The thick tree trunks grew closer together and blocked his view. He couldn't see much through the trees.

He rubbed Scout's thick neck and whispered, "I need you stay here. Okay? Stay."

Scout whined and pawed at Dakota's leg.

Dakota raised his voice enough to let the Lab know he was serious. "Stay."

Scout hung his head and lay down.

The dog didn't have to like it, but Allie had already lost Dixie. He'd do all he could to keep her partner safe. He waited to make sure Scout stayed in the down position, then Dakota crouched low and moved toward the light in the forest.

As he got closer, he had to belly crawl through the ash and dirt to stay out of the light's reach. Finally he spotted Ray, pacing in front of a lantern while he grumbled into his phone.

Just Ray, not an army. He walked in a flat clearing, his shadow from the LED lantern following him and bouncing off the stand of trees that surrounded the campfire ring in the middle.

But where was Allie?

Dakota moved slowly in a circle around the lit area. He stuck to Ray's back, but a couple of thick tree trunks blocked his view. Still no sign of Allie. He continued his crawl. His forearm landed on a thick branch, sending a loud crack into the air. Ray paused. Dakota froze.

He held his breath until Ray moved again. "I already told ya. I'm takin' care of it."

Was he talking to Earl? Maybe Dakota had been right that the two were connected—and now Ray was supposed to kill Allie and Dakota so Earl could get away with murder.

Not on my watch.

Dakota crawled to the closest rock outcropping. He stuck to the shadows and looped around to the other side of Ray's little camp. Then he saw her.

Allie sat on the ground, tied up and leaning against one of the big trees. But her eyes were closed, her head slumped down so her chin almost touched her shoulder. Dried blood trickled down her forehead.

The familiar rage boiled inside Dakota. But he needed to keep his wits about him and be smart.

Lord, help me to use my skills for good here. Help me save her.

Dakota took a full minute to study the area. Allie didn't stir. Her breathing seemed shallow. He pulled out the Glock and waited for Ray to make another pass and turn.

Go time.

He just prayed it wasn't too late.

THIRTEEN

ALLIE'S HEAD POUNDED. SHE SUCKED IN A BREATH, and pain lanced through her chest. Probably from where Ray had thrown her over his shoulder and then tossed her on the ground. She'd jarred her ribs landing on a rock. He'd knocked her good upside the head too. Maybe that was why it was so hard to open her eyes.

Cold night air pressed in on her, and she shivered.

She should've known Ray was lying. As soon as she was out of the car, he'd grabbed her. She tried to move her arm. It wouldn't budge. She pulled. Both hands were restrained.

"He's on his way. Once he's taken care of, she'll be joining him too."

Allie cracked her eyes open just enough to see a blurry image of Ray march behind the lantern on the ground. Her vision swirled, and she slammed her eyes shut again against the wave of nausea that hit.

"I think I know how to cover up my own tracks." He nearly spat the words at whoever he was talking to. "There'll be no trace of these two when I'm done."

She tried cracking her eyes open again and saw he had a phone in his hand.

"Whose fault is that? I wasn't the one who dumped Paulson out on that ranch. That's on you." Pause. "I know what I'm doing, Earl. If you'd done your part with the fire, Jen and the boys would have been taken care of too."

Nausea roiled in her stomach. The boys! *God, please keep them safe.*

"We'll take care of these two tonight and deal with them later—" He stopped. "Yeah. He'll show. I have the girl to make sure of that. And once he does, we won't have any more witnesses left." Pause. "Hey, you should be grateful I'm willing to help clean up your mess!"

Allie took a slow breath in and opened her eyes again. This time she was able to focus. Ray stuffed what looked like a satellite phone in his pocket and mumbled to himself.

She had to get away from him. Warn Jen and… Dakota.

Where was he?

He'll show. I have the girl to make sure of that.

This was a trap. Her hands were bound behind her back. Her ankles were duct-taped together.

Why had she pushed Dakota away thinking she was better off alone? He knew all about her horrific past and still wanted to give it a shot. What she wouldn't do to see him now. To tell him she was sorry for listening to her fears instead of giving them a chance. Because that's all it was. Fear of repeating the past. She might say she'd walked away for his sake, but it was glaringly obvious now. She'd done it because she believed the lie that she deserved it.

There's grace. Mercy. Loving kindness. Did you forget about those?

Belle's voice filled Allie's heart. She wasn't alone here. This wasn't a punishment. It was time for her to take stock of things. Because Belle was right. Allie was trying to pay back for one bad choice and debt she could never pay anyway.

All you can do is receive.

Okay then.

Lord, I need You.

Something rattled in the bushes just outside the ring of lantern light. Ray pulled a pistol out of his hip holster. He pointed it out in the dark. "I know you're out there, hotshot."

With a snarl and a flash of black fur, Scout leaped at Ray.

His powerful jaws clamped down on Ray's gun arm.

Ray dropped the pistol and roared. Someone else yelled, "No!"

Ray backhanded Scout's head. The dog released his arm and fell to the ground. He didn't move.

Allie screamed. "Scout!"

Ray charged her way, eyes boring into her filled with such hatred and darkness they looked like the pit of hell itself.

She braced for what he would do. Held her breath.

"Allie!" A dark form crashed out of the forest and lunged at Ray, knocking him down.

A blur of familiar red hair made Allie's breath catch. "Dakota!"

They hit the ground. Both men thrashed, tumbling

over each other as they grappled. Rolled. Grappled some more.

Dust flared up in a cloud.

Ray swung his arm, and Dakota's gun went flying. He grabbed Dakota and flipped him onto his back. The lantern toppled over and shattered, casting darkness about so Allie could barely see.

Dakota cried out.

She gasped. "No!"

Ray stood over Dakota, who grasped around in the dirt.

Something metallic glinted in the air.

"A knife," she screamed. "Ray has a knife!"

Dakota swung a gun up to face Ray right as the other man plunged the knife down toward him.

Three loud bangs sounded, flashing light so bright Allie could barely watch.

Ray staggered backward. The knife fell.

He clutched his chest, and blood blossomed on his shirt.

Dakota clambered to his feet, his chest heaving, the gun still pointed at Ray.

But the bigger man fell to the ground and didn't move.

Dakota kicked the knife away. He bent over and put fingers to Ray's neck, checking his pulse. But in the dim light of the moon, what looked like remorse and pain flashed on his handsome face.

Dakota staggered over to her with a flashlight now shining. He cut the tape at her ankles and then her wrists.

He fell forward but caught himself on the tree trunk. His moan went right to her heart.

"Kota, are you okay?" Allie rushed to him.

"Check…Scout." Dakota's breathing was labored. He sank to the ground and pointed over to the black Lab with his flashlight as he handed it to her.

Allie leaned over Scout's still body. He was breathing, at least.

"Scout? Do you hear me?"

His black nose twitched. He opened his eyes and raised his head.

"Hey, buddy. I'm here." She sank her fingers into the loose skin around his neck. She buried her nose in his fur and let the tears fall. "It's gonna be okay."

His tail gave a weak thump, and he allowed Allie to check him over while he lay there, watching her warily. She listened to his breathing. A little fast, but not horrible. She checked his gums. Normal. With a light hand, she scanned his body for wounds. "You doing okay, boy?"

He sat up, then stood. The Lab moved tentatively, but he could stand and walk on his own. That was a good sign.

Dakota, on the other hand, had his arm pressed against his stomach. She moved slowly over to him, fighting the dizziness. He didn't protest too much when Allie lifted his hand. "You're bleeding."

"Yeah. He caught me in the same side as my cut from the tree fall. Help me up."

"You're not going anywhere." She crawled over to where Ray's phone had fallen on the ground and called emergency dispatch.

He didn't fight her too much, which made the rumble of concern in her gut a full-on siren. But as they waited for help, there were a few things she wanted to get off her chest.

"You came back for me." She wiped the ash off

Dakota's forehead. Scout lay next to her, his snout resting on Dakota's leg.

"Of course I did." His face wrenched in pain, but he sat up. "But I shouldn't have left in the first place. I told you I'd be there for you, but I let you walk away."

She reached out, rested her palm against his chest. "You were right. I was too afraid to let anyone know the truth about what I'd done. I shut everyone out. Including you. But…if you think you can live with my past, with the consequences I can't change—"

He pulled her in closer, quieted her with a tender touch on her lips. His finger traced her bottom lip. Then her brow. His head dipped low, their foreheads together. "Just a chance, Allie. That's all I'm asking for. We can't change our pasts, but they don't have to define us either. And I think we could have a pretty awesome future together. What do you say?"

She closed the space between them, finally her lips on his. He kissed her back softly, as if savoring each point of contact.

Yeah, she could get used to this.

Scout sat up and barked.

Allie laughed. "Guess we know what Scout thinks."

"Smart dog." Dakota scrubbed Scout's blocky head.

"He is, isn't he? I always knew he had good instincts. But I believe we weren't finished yet." She leaned in for another kiss, this time wrapping both arms around his neck, her fingers tangling themselves in his hair as he met her passion with plenty of his own.

Dakota pulled back for a second. "You better watch out, Monroe. I'm falling hard for you."

"Glad it's not just me."

Because Dakota Masterson was better than any hero her imagination could come up with.

Now that Dakota had had a taste of the sweetness that was Allie, he couldn't get out of this hospital room fast enough. He finished dressing. How much longer was the doctor gonna take? He wanted to see Allie. No, he *needed* to see her. Needed to see that he hadn't imagined that kiss at the campground. That she was really here, waiting for him.

He paced the small exam room. Slowly. Every muscle in his body hurt, but he didn't have to stay overnight.

Thanks for the small mercies as well as the big ones, Lord.

Now that he was stitched up, he was ready to go.

Dakota was about to flag down the nearest medical professional when the nurse knocked and came in. She handed him a stack of papers.

"All right, since we can't talk you into staying overnight, here are your discharge papers. But the doctor needs to know where you want your prescription for pain meds to be sent. Do you use a pharmacy here in Ember?"

"Not necessary. I'll stick with ibuprofen."

She wrinkled her nose. "Are you sure? You have bruised ribs, stitches, not to mention the injuries to your hands and face."

"No thanks. I don't do so well with narcotics."

"All right. Then sign here and you're free to go."

He scribbled his signature on the tablet she handed him and walked out to the waiting room.

Allie's smile lit up as soon as she saw him. Looked like she'd been checked out too. Her head was wrapped with gauze, and she had a nice shiner, but she was still the most beautiful woman he knew. She rushed over and hugged him. Scout barked.

"You want a little attention too, huh?" Dakota reached down and scratched the dog behind his ears.

"We've been waiting for you. Everything is okay?"

"Yeah. I'm good. You?"

"Doc said I'm fine. And..."

Dakota stayed kneeling by Scout. "And what?"

"I talked to my dad. And Mom."

"You did?" He stood, reached for her hand. "How did it go?"

Her eyes shimmered with tears. "I got the whole story out, and by the end I think we were all crying. Somehow, my dad knew, or at least suspected a lot of the details already."

"So they didn't kick you out of the family?"

She wiped the tears that had fallen. "No. They were just waiting for me to come back home, in a sense. They said I was already forgiven and that nothing changes how much they love me."

"I told you." He smirked.

Allie rolled her eyes at him. "I know. Go ahead and rub it in." She paused. "I think I'll spend some time with them before I head back to Benson. And maybe when you're done for the season or have some time off, you can come with me to meet them."

Dakota's heart swelled. "I'd like that." Before he could say more, Scout pawed at their legs until

Dakota bent down and rubbed his flanks. "Is someone feeling neglected?"

The dog licked his cheek.

"All right, Scout. My turn. Lie down." Allie waited for Scout to obey—which he did the first time! Then she stood on her tiptoes and planted a sweet lingering kiss on Dakota's lips.

"Now that is the best medicine a guy could ask for. But be careful. I might get addicted."

"I think that suits me just fine." She kissed him again.

"That's enough of that, you two." Kane sauntered in twirling his keys. "Since neither one of you is supposed to be driving, guess I get to be your chauffeur. You ready to head to the sheriff's office? They want your statements."

"Let's get out of here." Dakota kept his good arm around Allie as they walked out to the truck. "Did they find the boys?"

Allie nodded. "They're safe and sound with their aunt. And Jen is still here in the hospital. She said she'll move in with her sister for a while until they get settled and find a new place to live."

"Good. And Earl?" Dakota asked.

Kane opened the truck door for Allie. "From what I hear, he's still out there. Are you leaving the hotshots to look for him?"

"No, although the doctor wants me off the crew for the week until I get my stitches out. Maybe I'll do a little investigating while I'm recovering." Dakota hefted himself up gently into the truck.

Allie sat in the middle, while Kane drove. "What about you, Allie. You sticking around?"

She looked over at Dakota and took his hand.

"Yeah. I've still got some training to do for Scout. And you never know when a search and rescue dog will come in handy."

Kane turned out of the parking lot. "Yeah, there's something strange going on around here. I feel like we're just hitting the tip of the iceberg. So count me in on whatever you two are investigating. Someone's gotta watch your six."

Allie chuckled. "Yeah, especially with all the trouble Dakota seems to find."

"Trouble? Me?" Dakota gave her a look of mock innocence.

"Oh, I knew you were trouble the first time I saw you." She gave him a pointed look.

He leaned over and whispered in her ear. "Yeah, but you like it."

"Maybe." Her eyes lit with a mischievous glint. A pause. "Okay, fine. I do."

She kissed him until Kane cleared his throat. "All right, all right. That's enough, you two. I said I'd chauffeur, not chaperone."

Allie laughed. Dakota smiled. Flashing back to where he'd been a year and a half ago, in the throes of his addiction, he couldn't have imagined this was where he'd end up. A hotshot firefighter. An incredible woman wanting him to meet her family. A man humbled and broken but now, somehow, so much stronger because he knew what it meant to depend on God. Every day was a blank slate. And he had plenty of family, brothers and sisters in Christ, to help and serve.

How did that old hymn go?

Praise the Lord, praise the Lord, O my soul.

Thank you for reading *Flashback*! Gear up for the next Chasing Fire: Montana romantic suspense thriller, *Firestorm* by Lisa Phillips. Turn the page for a sneak peek!

SECRETS. BETRAYAL. SACRIFICE.
THIS TIME, THEY'RE NOT JUST FIGHTING FIRE.

He thought his life was over…and then she walked back in.

Charlie Benning has always been a rescuer—first with the Last Chance County Fire and Rescue team, and now as a firefighter with the Jude County Hotshots. But this summer isn't about saving lives—it's about hiding his own terrible secret. A secret he's keeping from his estranged daughter, Alexis.

But fate is about to intervene.

Will their secrets destroy their second chance?

Jayne Price raised her son, Orion, on her own just fine, thank you. And now, she runs Wildlands Academy, a summer camp that teaches kids how to fight forest fires and confront their own teenage angst—kids like Alexis Benning, who clearly has a chip on her shoulder about her semi-estranged, firefighter father.

And Jayne has her own issues, like not wanting her only son to join the elite smokejumping corps. It's enough that he's risking his life as a hotshot on the Jude County team.

Then the wildfire turns its force onto the camp and suddenly the hotshots show up to help her fight it. Only problem...the last person she expects is for her former flame, Charlie Benning—the man she can't forget—to show up working alongside her son.

Rather, *his* son.

Who he doesn't know exists.

And then Charlie discovers the secret she's been keeping, and he's torn between anger and the long-simmering love that refuses to die. And Jayne isn't about to let go of the man she loves a second time. But if the blazing wildfire isn't enough, a dangerous and relentless killer is on the prowl in the woods...

Now, with the camp cut off from the outside world and the fire closing in, it's a race against time as

Charlie, Jayne, Orion, and a team of courageous smokejumpers join forces to protect the campers against a merciless inferno and a murderer. But the biggest threat of all might be Charlie's devastating secret that could destroy the happy ending they've waited for so long.

Prepare for an edge-of-your-seat journey that will leave you breathless until the very last page, in book four of the Chasing Fire: Montana series.

FIRESTORM

CHASING FIRE: MONTANA | BOOK 4

CHAPTER 1

Everything was going according to plan.

Kind of.

Firefighter Charlie Benning stared down the flames, then turned and swung his axe at the tree. If they didn't get this line cut, the fire would jump to the trees on the other side of the deer trail and spread toward residences.

So long as the wind didn't change, they had a shot at containing this fire so it didn't destroy any more of the Kootenai National Forest. In the last week, the blaze had nearly doubled in size. It was spreading north and had split into two forks, with the western tine headed for the town of Snowhaven.

He lifted his axe again.

Pain ripped through his side at his lower back. He hissed and barely managed to keep the axe from flying at one of the other hotshots on this team.

"Whoa." Kane, one of the "Trouble Boys" as they'd been dubbed by the others, grabbed the axe handle. "Easy there." The guy had close-shaved dark-blond hair and eyes one of the female hotshots had described as brooding.

Charlie grunted. "I'm good." But he let Kane take the axe. That guy's broody eyes saw way too much, and Charlie had been avoiding anything personal since the fire season started.

It wasn't time to slip up now. Not when the fire had grown big enough that his plan had a shot at working. The alternative would be messy. This had to go one way.

"Why don't you take a water break?" Kane turned and hammered at the tree with more strength than Charlie had even back when he was in his twenties. He was over the hill of four and zero now—a fact the hotshots insisted on reminding him of every day, calling him "old man" and "grandpa."

Might've bothered him before, but not lately.

Charlie walked off the pain as he headed for the water barrel Hammer had carried out here. The fellow hotshot went by Ham most of the time, and he saw way too much with that military situational awareness he wore like a coat.

Everyone knew walking something off didn't work. Not when the doctor had used words like *chronic* and *dialysis*.

He'd left Last Chance County before that conversation could turn to *stage two* or *failure*. Then he'd fudged the medical part of acceptance onto the hotshot crew—bypassing rookie training with the courses he'd taken over the years as a firefighter. He knew what he was doing. The truth would come out eventually, but that would be after the fact.

Too late.

Charlie might have had a decorated career in

rescue squad, but he also had a failed marriage and an estranged daughter he'd dropped off at the teen firefighter camp up in the mountains. Wildlands Academy would be her home for the summer, and at the end of the season, Charlie would have done what he needed to do.

Everything would be taken care of.

Charlie patted the letter in his bulky fire-pants pocket, tucked next to the shelter he was supposed to never have to deploy.

"You good?" The boss lifted his chin. Conner Young was a good man, a family guy like Charlie would never be.

He lifted his chin in reply. "Probably just pulled a muscle." He got a drink, wishing for a moment of solitude he could use to take a pill, and turned to watch the hotshot crew.

Two women, seven men, not including him. The two youngest guys were in their early twenties—which made him old enough to be their father.

A thought that didn't make him feel more spry.

"I checked the weather report this morning. If that front comes over from the coast like they think, the fire could change directions and head to the firefighter camp, Wildlands Academy." Charlie pulled a map from his pants pocket and unfolded it.

Conner nodded. "I'm waiting for Miles to confirm, but I think we'll get redeployed after this to head up there."

Charlie marked the path of the wind. If it came in from the west, it could funnel through a valley that would lead right to the camp north of them.

Orion Price lowered his Pulaski and headed over. The guy was twenty-two but had more experience as a hotshot than most of the crew. The kid had gel in his dark-blond hair and features that were familiar even though Charlie had never met him before this summer.

Now that he knew who Orion's mother was, it made sense.

The guy said, "Not sure we need to worry about the academy. They'll be protected even if the fire heads in that direction. It was designed that way, and Mom keeps the vegetation cut back."

"Yeah?" Charlie liked the kid. Not too much of a know-it-all, and not so quiet like the youngest hotshot, Mack, that he never said a word.

Conner said, "Jayne knows what she's doing."

Her name cut through him like someone had taken their Pulaski and hammered it into him. Didn't matter that he knew she lived there and ran Wildlands Academy now. She hadn't been there the day he'd dropped off his daughter Alexis. That was the way he'd designed it. Purposely, so he didn't run into Jayne.

Jayne Price, the girl he'd loved at seventeen and walked away from—never looking back. Orion's mother. The woman who ran the teen firefighter camp. He would never *not* react to her.

And whatever odd expression was on his face hadn't gone unnoticed. *Quit thinking about her.*

Orion frowned at him. "She's been working at the camp since before I was born. It's a fire safety camp. The whole place was designed to keep from catching fire, even if it's completely surrounded by flames. The trees are at least thirty feet back from the cabins and the main house. There's a lake to the west, so they can get a quick water drop if necessary."

Charlie managed to nod. "And your dad?" He hadn't asked yet. As if he wanted to know that she was happily married now. Or that Orion loved his dad in a way Alexis would never feel about him. Charlie shook off the thoughts. He was the one who'd walked away from her at the end of the summer and gone home to Last Chance County. He hoped she had been happy all these years.

Orion shrugged. "Don't have one. Never have."

Oof. Sore subject much? Charlie didn't need to care about Jayne's love life—which was apparently as good as his had been in the twenty years since they'd seen each other. The thing he'd had with Alexis's mother had been a bad idea from start to finish. They'd both made it worse, and Alexis had suffered in the middle. So Charlie had opted to make himself scarce versus making it harder for his daughter with all the friction between him and her mother.

Charlie said, "I dropped off my daughter Alexis at the camp at the beginning of summer. I'm going to worry."

"Have you called her, asked her what they can see of the fire?"

He tried not to stiffen at Conner's question, just saying, "Uh, no. Haven't been able to get through. Ry, what about your mom? Have you checked in with her recently?"

The son of the woman he had never quit thinking about blinked. "I…uh." Orion cleared his throat. "We had a fight. Right at the beginning of the season. She doesn't even know I broke up with Laina over Memorial Day weekend."

Conner set a hand on Orion's shoulder. "You haven't spoken to her at all?"

The kid shrugged it off. "She hasn't called me either."

Charlie wanted to tell the guy to suck it up and make amends, but that would make him the biggest hypocrite west of Denver. He'd sent Alexis two texts at the beginning of summer, but his seventeen-year-old hadn't replied.

They'd been estranged since before his ex-wife had lost out to her protracted battle with cancer. Now Alexis was grieving the loss of her mother, and he had to figure out how to get her to let him be her father with the time he had left.

He didn't know how to fix that. But he could fix the rest of it.

If he got everything to go as planned.

"Whoa." One of the guys yelled from behind them, about fifteen feet away.

"Houston!" That was Emily who'd screamed.

Charlie turned to watch her scramble back, falling as she moved away from what had everyone's attention. Houston had vanished into the earth in the center of a circle of hotshots. A cave-in, or some kind of sink hole?

Hammer got down on his stomach and inched forward. The ground in front of him caved in, and the whole area rumbled under them. Charlie got closer to the hole, grabbing Mack's arm when he started toward his brother. "Don't become another victim." To the group he said, "Everyone take a step back. Ham, stay where you are."

"I can see him." The guy was military. It wasn't something a guy like Ham could hide. His history of service was there in the way he walked, the way he focused right now.

Kane and Saxon, his buddies, hid it better. Mack appeared to be along for the ride as Ham's kid brother. They regularly orbited Sanchez—the female hotshot—in a way that looked an awful lot like they were a protective detail.

They certainly had secrets. Maybe one day the world would discover what they were, but it wouldn't be today.

"Stay where you are." Charlie knelt by Ham's feet and tried to see into the hole Houston had fallen into. All he saw was the top of Houston's bald head and the nasty burn scars he had on one side of his face. Charlie called out, "Hey, Pastor! You good?"

No reply.

He patted Ham's leg. "Tell me what you can see."

"Shoulder. Side of his head." Where those burn scars were. "No blood. But he's pretty buried. It's covering his chest and lower body. Not sure if he's breathing."

"He's not too far down." Charlie turned to the group. "Rope. We need to rappel in and pull him out."

"Whoever goes down will end up being buried with dirt like Houston." Orion pulled on his gloves. "Then we'll have two victims."

Charlie said, "That's why we're going to hook in and use a pulley system to get them both out. Houston, and whoever goes down after him."

Saxon stared at the hole with his dark gaze and those Middle Eastern features. "Looks like a tunnel down there."

Orion huffed. "I suppose you want to be the hero, Charlie?"

So everyone could realize he wasn't able to do the

things he'd done every day with rescue squad in Last Chance County? Nope. "You want this, Ry?"

Orion nodded.

"Then hook up. We need to get Houston out before more dirt piles on him and we have to call Sophie and tell her we lost him."

Conner gave Charlie a dark look. Charlie ignored it and got to work, organizing everyone so there were guys holding the rope as Orion went in. He had the kid tie another loop around Houston, under his arms. Team two pulled Houston while team one pulled out Orion.

"Let me see him." Charlie knelt beside Houston and tugged off one glove. He felt for a pulse, then checked Houston's breathing. He patted his friend's cheek. "Don't make me call home and tell the chief his brother fell through a hole in the ground."

Houston pulled in a breath and coughed. Dirt expelled from between his lips.

Charlie let out a breath. "There you are."

"Don't tell Macon."

Charlie chuckled. "That goes both ways, brother."

"Deal." Houston sat up, groaning.

Conner said, "Charlie, Orion, take Houston back to town in my truck. Get him checked out at the hospital. The rest of us will finish up here and hit the bus. We're getting redeployed to the north edge of the fire so we can cut it off from up there." Then he pointed at the sky.

A series of parachutes dropped from a plane to the north, always a sight to see. The Ember smokejumpers had been sent in, probably to contain the blaze from the north and push back against the edge before it ravaged the entire county.

Charlie picked out his lieutenant, Logan Crawford, in the middle of the line. He heard someone mutter a prayer for their protection.

Conner clapped his gloves together. "Let's move out."

"Let's get that pile cleared away!" Jayne Price pointed at the stack of brush the kids had cleared. This area to the east of a fire road an hour's walk from Wildlands Academy hadn't been cut back in weeks. "Down to the road. Okay, guys?"

"On it." A couple of teen boys, normally eager, walked a lot slower now. The Masterson twins from Benson, whose parents worked search and rescue, had jumped at every challenge she and her staff had presented to them. But it had been a long day.

All in all they had fifteen kids, a mix of male and female. Right now all of them were tired and dirty, probably sick of sucking in the gray air. Most had given up brushing falling ash from their clothes and hair.

They had a couple of guys from town that came out with them on field trips or came up to camp and taught classes. One was a crusty old firefighter who'd fought blazes in the sixties and seventies. The other had been a smokejumper, and the kids always sat riveted, listening to stories of jumping out of planes to fight fire.

They'd all been out here for hours, working like hotshots to slow the spread of a fire that might come this direction.

Thanks to the way God had carved this canyon,

the smoke hung above them like a ceiling of cloud. But they wouldn't be able to stay out here much longer when the air quality was so bad. Not without suffering long-term effects—the way her grandpa had. She could hear that wet-rattle cough in her mind even though he'd died when she was much younger than these kids.

She strode down the line, her boots kicking up the dusty earth.

"Doesn't look good." Her administrator walked over to meet her. Bridget Willis had been working at the camp since back when Jayne had been one of these kids—the summer her life had flipped upside down. A story she'd broken down and decided to tell the kids last night over the cooking fire while their dinner hot dogs sizzled. All because two of her campers had been caught sneaking off.

Not unheard of—after all, it was what Jayne had done. Then it was what Logan and one of the camp girls had done years after, and so many others. She'd seen Logan in the grocery store at the beginning of summer, and they'd had a good ole laugh about that.

But it wasn't funny.

Even if she had Orion as a result, she didn't need more parents complaining to her that their kids had spent summer at her camp and learned more than just wildland firefighting. Wildlands Academy was about learning to be a hotshot. Building strength of mind and body—and strength of character.

Bridget, in her fifties and more comfortable in a library, glanced at the smoke to the west. She'd surprised Jayne from the beginning with her brand new hiking boots and a smile that never got tired.

"That weather report didn't do it justice. The wind is picking up."

Jayne nodded. "Let's get this brush in the truck and head to the river. They might get up close and personal with the fire tonight, but it won't jump the water."

One of the girls walked by her. Alexis Martin, one of the older teens, had been giving her the cold shoulder all morning. The girl glanced aside at Jayne when she thought Jayne wasn't looking, peering between the strands of the brown curls that fell to her shoulders.

Because of the story Jayne had told them all? Her cautionary tale of why hookups were a bad idea. She had no idea why the seventeen-year-old reacted that way over Jayne's sordid tale of a summer romance and discovering two months later that she was pregnant. She'd kept the tale youth-group friendly, but teens responded better when she was "real" with them, and that meant being honest about why she had a grown son and no husband.

About the boy named Charlie who had swept her into what had felt like a dream.

Bridget clapped her hands together. "Listen up, everyone! We're heading to the river."

More than one teen groaned.

"We know you're tired," Jayne called out. "But the wind is picking up, and if it changes direction, we could end up in trouble."

They were all kitted out in fire gear. They knew what to do in a disaster scenario—each one had a fire shelter. Safety was a nonnegotiable for her.

"I've never lost a firefighter, and I won't break that streak today. So we push to the river, and then we break out the soap and get cleaned up. Who wants my famous spicy gumbo for dinner? Maybe we can do those hot ham and cheese sandwiches tomorrow."

That picked up a few spirits. Thankfully Jayne had set it up in the slow cooker back in the camp lodge before they'd come out this morning, so it should be about ready. They were going to camp out overnight, but that didn't mean not eating well.

They just had to get to a good spot.

She said, "S'mores for dessert."

That got the rest of them moving.

Bridget said, "Let's get this brush to the truck so I can go pick up dinner from camp and bring it out."

"I'll take a pepperoni pizza." One of the guys grinned—Mr. Romance, who'd convinced Shelly from California (not Shelly from Alaska) to sneak off into the bushes with him last night after bed down. Jayne had spotted them more than once, and it was why she'd decided to tell the story.

"I'll get right on that." Bridget grinned.

The crew started grabbing bundles of brush and walking down the trail to the truck they had on hand for emergencies and supply delivery. Other than that, they were alone out here. Carrying what they needed, and walking from camp nearly ten miles to the northwest.

Most years there were a few fires they could help put out by clearing lines hotshots had already dug to keep this area safe, all the while praying the fire stayed far away and even that it might head in another direction entirely.

It didn't look like that prayer would be answered today, so she asked for wisdom instead and protection for the kids—and all the firefighters. Not just her son

Orion, but every one of them, and the smokejumpers she'd seen parachute overhead a bit ago.

She wasn't a stranger to unanswered prayers.

God didn't say yes to everything, and why should He when He knew far better than she did? If the wind blew the fire toward them and the camp, then the outcome would be in His hands.

Jayne tugged on the hem of each glove, then picked up a bundle of brush in her arms and raced one of the kids to the truck parked on the fire road a quarter mile to the north.

Alexis dumped her load in the truck bed beside Jayne's.

Jayne caught her attention as they turned. "Everything okay?"

The girl shot her an odd look. "Sure." Alexis brushed hair back from her face and wound up with a smear of dirt on her forehead. "Your son…the one you mentioned. Does he ever come around the camp?"

"Sometimes." Jayne wasn't going to lie to the girl. "We actually had a pretty big fight at the beginning of the fire season." Her stomach clenched and she looked at the thirty-foot pine trees that stood in two rows flanking the fire road. "He wants to be a smokejumper. That's…it's actually what killed my dad. His parachute failed."

Alexis studied her, entirely too much pain in her eyes. She'd suffered loss, but for the most part refused to talk about it.

"Who did you lose?"

Alexis said, "My mom died right after Christmas. Couple days before New Year. She had cancer."

"I'm sorry for your loss."

The girl winced. "It was..." She shrugged. "I don't even know. It was bad for a long time. But she wasn't a nice person, which sounds like a horrible thing to say about someone who's dead."

"All we can do is be honest about how we feel." Jayne set a hand on the girl's shoulder. "God knows it before we even come to Him, but He wants us to talk to Him. To build that relationship and rely on Him for our comfort and strength. It sounds hard, but it's actually very simple."

Jayne had no idea where the girl was with faith. She made no secret of the way she guided the kids. If they needed help or advice, it was going to be based on the Bible—the book Jayne had lived her life by since Orion was born and she'd realized he needed more than she could give him.

The teen shook her head. "There's nothing simple about this."

Alexis had said her father had custody of her and that he was a hotshot in Ember for the summer. With the exception of the time since yesterday, when she'd told her teenage love story, Alexis had been her right-hand girl so far this summer. In a lot of ways, she'd come to rely on the teen, who had some basic medical training and a lifeguard certification and was planning on getting an EMT certificate next year in her senior year of high school. The girl was going to make something of her life, even if none of the adults she had watching out for her had ever encouraged her to do it.

Alexis was going places, and she didn't need anyone's help. Maybe it was worry for her father that had Alexis out of sorts. If she were Jayne's daughter, Jayne would be proud of the way she carried on after her mother passed and her father dumped her here for the summer so he could join the Jude County Hotshots. The way she was proud of Orion and the good he was doing in the world every day, not just during fire season. Her son had grown up to be a good man.

Despite who his father was.

"I'm gonna go help with the rest." Alexis wandered off toward the brush that still needed clearing.

Jayne checked on everyone and kept one eye on the clouds in the distance as she did it, then she looked at her phone to see if there were any new updates.

It chimed as she pulled it from her belt holster, and she sucked in a breath. *It's worse than I thought.* The text from Miles and the update from the National Interagency Fire Center in Idaho was a double alert—and they needed to respond in double time.

"Hustle up, everyone! Change of dinner plans. The camp has been upgraded to 'Ready to go' status. We need to get back there and be prepared to evacuate."

Looking for more more exciting romantic suspense from Sunrise Publishing?

DON'T MISS ANY CHASING FIRE: MONTANA STORIES

With heart-pounding excitement, gripping suspense, and sizzling (but clean!) romance, the CHASING FIRE: MONTANA series, brought to you by the incredible authors of Sunrise Publishing, including the dynamic duo of bestselling authors Susan May Warren and Lisa Phillips, is your epic summer binge read.

Immerse yourself in a world of short, captivating novels that are designed to be devoured in one sitting.

Each book is a standalone masterpiece, (no story cliffhangers!) although you'll be craving the next one in the series!

Follow the Montana Hotshots and Smokejumpers as they chase a wildfire through northwest Montana. The pages ignite with clean romance and high-stakes danger—these heroes (and heroines!) will capture your heart. The biggest question is...who will be your summer book boyfriend?

A BREED APART: LEGACY UNLEASHED!

Experience the high-octane thrills, danger, and romance in Ronie Kendig's A Breed Apart: Legacy series.

MORE ADVENTURE AWAITS...

FIND THEM ALL AT SUNRISE PUBLISHING!

ACKNOWLEDGMENTS

I'm pretty sure somewhere I heard a saying, something about it taking a village to bring a book into the world. I leaned heavily on my village for this one!

To my amazing editors and the two that plotted to bring their fictional worlds colliding together, Lisa Phillips and Susan May Warren, thank you for including me on this wild ride. You are both a tremendous support! I want to be like you two when I grow up. 😉

To my literal village here in Upsala, you are so encouraging as I tread this writing journey. Especially my hometown super-readers and besties: Wanda Erickson, Linda Day, Lisa Day, Bethany Malisheske, Karen Hoffman, Sarah Thomas, Angela Hollermann, and so many others! And a special shout out to the Upsala Public Library and Friends of the Library. You are the best cheerleaders!

To my tiny but mighty writers village of Mollie Rushmeyer, Andrea Christenson, and Rachel Russell, in what has been such a difficult year, you have been right by my side. I couldn't have done this without you! I love our writing sessions and support group meetings and texts. This road is a lot smoother (and less lonely) because of you three.

To my prayer huddle…your prayers upheld me from beginning to end.

And to my most important village, my family, you put up with a lot for me to do this, and I don't take that for granted. No matter how many books I write I will never be able to adequately express how important you are to me. "Love" just doesn't encompass it all, but until I can find a better word, I love you forever and day, Jesse, Anders, Evie, Lucy, and Trygg.

ABOUT MICHELLE SASS ALECKSON

After growing up on both the east and west coasts, **Michelle Sass Aleckson** now lives the country life in central Minnesota with her own hero and their four kids. She loves rocking out to 80's music on a Saturday night, playing Balderdash with the fam, and getting lost in good stories. Especially stories that shine grace. And if you're wondering, yes, Sass is her maiden name. Visit her at www.michellealeckson.com.

facebook.com/AuthorMichelleAleckson
instagram.com/michelle_aleckson
x.com/MchelleAleckson
goodreads.com/michellealeckson
bookbub.com/authors/michelle-sass-aleckson
amazon.com/stores/Michelle-Sass-Aleckson/author/B08M8P51B7

ALSO BY MICHELLE SASS ALECKSON

ROMANTIC SUSPENSE

Hidden Ranch Peril

CONTEMPORARY ROMANCE

The Way You Love Me

Crazy for You

Right Here Waiting

Once Upon A Winter Wonderland

CONNECT WITH SUNRISE

Thank you again for reading *Flashback*. We hope you enjoyed the story. If you did, would you be willing to do us a favor and leave a review? It doesn't have to be long—just a few words to help other readers know what they're getting. (But no spoilers! We don't want to wreck the fun!) Thank you again for reading!

We'd love to hear from you—not only about this story, but about any characters or stories you'd like to read in the future. Contact us at www.sunrisepublishing.com/contact.

We also have a monthly update that contains sneak peeks, reviews, upcoming releases, and fun stuff for our reader friends. Sign up at www.sunrisepublishing.com or scan our QR code.

MORE EPIC ROMANTIC ADVENTURE

CHASING FIRE: MONTANA

Flashpoint by Susan May Warren

Flashover by Megan Besing

Flashback by Michelle Sass Aleckson

Firestorm by Lisa Phillips

Fireline by Kate Angelo

Fireproof by Susan May Warren

MONTANA FIRE BY SUSAN MAY WARREN

Where There's Smoke (Summer of Fire)

Playing with Fire (Summer of Fire)

Burnin' For You (Summer of Fire)

Oh, The Weather Outside is Frightful (Christmas novella)

I'll be There (Montana Fire/Deep Haven crossover)

Light My Fire (Summer of the Burning Sky)

The Heat is On (Summer of the Burning Sky)

Some Like it Hot (Summer of the Burning Sky)

You Don't Have to Be a Star (spin-off)

LAST CHANCE FIRE AND RESCUE BY LISA PHILLIPS

Expired Return

Expired Hope (with Megan Besing)

Expired Promise (with Emilie Haney)

Expired Vows (with Laura Conaway)

LAST CHANCE COUNTY BY LISA PHILLIPS

Expired Refuge

Expired Secrets

Expired Cache

Expired Hero

Expired Game

Expired Plot

Expired Getaway

Expired Betrayal

Expired Flight

Expired End

Made in the USA
Columbia, SC
08 July 2024